Jimmy this, Jimmy that

Michael Shand

Published by Dolman Scott in 2016

Copyright ©Michael Shand 2016

All rights reserved. No part of this publication may be reproduced, stored in a retrieval system, or transmitted in any form or by any means, electronic, mechanical, photocopy, recording or otherwise, without prior written permission of the copyright owner. Nor can it be circulated in any form of binding or cover other than that in which it is published and without similar condition including this condition being imposed on a subsequent purchaser

ISBN 978-1-909204-99-7

Dolman Scott
www.dolmanscott.com

Michael Shand is a Playwright and Novelist, born in 1981. His stage play *Depravity* won an *Arts Trust of Scotland* award in 2012 and subsequently made the Shortlist for the *Script Space Competition*. Michael has also been on the Shortlist for the *New Playwrights Award*. He lives in Edinburgh with his wife, Sara, and his son, Charlie. **Jimmy this, Jimmy that** is his debut novel.

This book is dedicated to friendships past and present.

Acknowledgments:

My wife *Sara Rodger-Shand,* **My son** *Charlie Rodger-Shand,* **My mum** *Joyce Gunn Cairns,* **My editor** *Claire Wingfield*

Contents

Prologue xiii

Jimmy 1

this 105

Jimmy 115

that 189

Jimmy this, Jimmy that

Prologue

There's a gentle feeling of liberation that emerges when standing at a bus stop.

For a matter of minutes the bus tracker becomes the most important entity in your life. The numbers become your salvation; 6 minutes…5…4…3.

A packed 16 on a Monday morning; employees rushing to clock-in, all iPhones, iPods, Apple Laptops and e-readers, squashed against schoolbags and hooped earrings and a twelve year old who thinks it's acceptable to play their music so loud even the bus driver can bob along to it. For a book reader like me, of actual physical pages, it can become a bit too much to handle.

The little granny standing beside me tugs at my arm. Which bus is approaching? 'The 16 pal. Just jump on my shoulders.' She smiles in that delicate and thankful manner older people enjoy.

Thriving in my moment of approved cordiality, I allow her to get on the bus before me, almost instantly regretting it when she tells the driver he looks like her son, though as a true Edinburgh bus driver he merely acknowledges her with a smile.

Just as I'm depositing my £1.50, something written on the wall across the street catches my eye: in large blue writing someone has scribbled ***Jimmy is an Arsehole.***

After taking my ticket, I sit, fixing my eyes on that writing; taking in the moment, the memory, and the history.

As the bus pulls away, so does the name.

The interesting thing about the past is that it never really goes away. Lingering like a bad smell or an uninvited guest. It always seems to be present – even in its most trivial form. Just like when you take an old painting off the wall and the colours, the contours, *the feeling* all remaining an existential part of your home.

Memories don't just disappear, and every so often, whether we're prepared for it or not, the world will quite appositely find a way to trigger certain moments from our past.

*

Jimmy Stokes was a right arsehole. That's why he got stabbed that time on the field. He was my mate though.

For a while.

Jimmy was the only one in the young team who carried a blade. Imagined a knife was a necessity; an extended part of the human body; an essential part of everyday living.

You hang about with people like him when you're younger. People who think they're iconic, but are really moronic. Jimmy thought he was the quintessential gangster, but in truth, he was actually just the quintessential bully. Fitted the stereotype perfectly. Small but bulky, unhealthy complexion, a distant look of anger permanently dominating his countenance. Didn't have the suit jackets, the cars, the warehouses full of cocaine, or even a secret compartment for his weapons. There was just himself, in his own little destructive world.

Like most bullies, you did have to afford him a slight modicum of reverence – on the outside anyway – because if you looked at him the wrong way, he'd threaten to slash your dad's car tyres or break into your house. Or even worse: stab you with his blade.

In some ways I was envious of Jimmy Stokes. His confidence, his swagger, his unearned respect, his time moving in and out the vagina, and even the way other teenagers tip-toed around him. I always lamented these feelings when they materialised though, because, in truth, the guy was a fucking idiot, and didn't deserve even the most infinitesimal notion of anyone's envy.

So, why were we mates? Why spend almost every day in his company? Why did we not just ditch him for someone better?

An embryo grows inside the womb, and when the baby is born, everyone congratulates its safe arrival: how wonderful and cute it is. What they never say is that this is just the beginning, the rudimentary stage. This little thing will have to evolve through time. It will have to learn about the world by making mistakes, choosing the wrong path, and fighting the wrong battles.

The difference between the past and the present is this; if someone like Jimmy Stokes said to me in the street nowadays, 'Smash that windy or A'l fuckin smash you,' I'd probably laugh, or better still, phone the police. Obviously I'd be struggling with a feeling of trepidation, but I certainly wouldn't do it.

But fear is a very difficult emotion to understand.

Jimmy this, Jimmy that

It took me until at least my twenties to realise the extremity of arseholeness surrounding a guy like Jimmy Stokes. By then he was long gone.

A few feet underground, creating havoc in the afterlife.

Didn't half leave behind a plethora of barbaric incidents, though. Talk about leaving your mark on history.

*

There were four of us; Me, Jimmy, Noggin, and Specks. I was quite an ordinary teenager. The inconspicuous one in the crowd, just tagging along, relatively fortunate in my parenting. Dad had a decent job as an electrician, and mum a couple of cleaning jobs for the rich families on Anne Street. Although my dad always drank at the weekend and never failed to stumble through the door calling my mum all the names under the son, he never raised his hand to her.

Not sure if I could say the same for some of our neighbours, though. The screaming in the night will forever reside in my bones.

Jimmy was the type of teenager all the neighbours talked about. Dad in and out of jail. Mum permanently hanging out the window with a fag stuck to her lips and a bottle of vodka clutched to her swaying arms. Court citations regular as the postman. You always knew when his dad wasn't inside; just had to check his mums face for bruises.

What hope did he have, really?

Jimmy this, Jimmy that

Noggin got his nickname because of a small birthmark on his spam. Born with it, right in the middle of his forehead. Wore a hat, or grew his fringe pretty long. In a lot of ways he was a bit incongruous in our group. Had an obvious self-assurance and integrity that we never enjoyed. Unlike me, he only really smoked and drank when Jimmy forced it on him. Parents both had fairly decent jobs. You always felt the word opportunity would float in his direction and sidestep the rest of us.

No, I'm not entirely sure how a guy like Noggin ended up kicking about with us, but all I can say is this: I'm glad he did.

Specks, who got his nickname for obvious reasons was the quiet one. Jimmy used to kick him up and down the streets – much to the disgust of Noggin and I. He never fought back: always refused to lower himself to Jimmy's level. I didn't have particularity high hopes for his future, but I always really admired Specks for what he put up with, for enduring Jimmy's darkest side. I say darkest because his personality had no light. It went from dark to darkest.

I'll never forget the time Specks got into a fight with a naturally better built and hugely more respected guy from the year above us called Briggs. After Specks got on top of him, he attempted to scratch the guys' eyes out, all the time muttering, 'Fuck you Jimmy, Fuck you.'

He was the master thief, our Specks: a legend in the stealing game. People refused to believe this little geeky looking boy with glasses was capable of anything suspicious. Of course, he took full advantage of this prejudice. Shops, cars, houses, caravans, even your laundry wasn't safe.

One day, Jimmy said he would look favourably on him if he stole knickers from this man's washing line, and then go to his door and ask if he fancied buying some pants at a cut price. Obviously he didn't use the word 'favourably,' but believe it or not, he actually did it, whilst we stood on the street corner, watching with a mixture of awe and gratefulness for not being in his shoes. I'll never forget the look on the guys face when he opened his door and Specks said, 'alrite mate, yer wife wantae buy some cheap pants?' Best part about it was he actually bought them; probably to stop him doing it again or maybe just because he couldn't believe the audacity of the little bastard.

*

So that was the gang in our prime. Stood about street corners as though we owned them; spitting, swearing, and intimidating anyone who passed by. All that really mattered was that every day was different. From the morning, when I opened my front door, to the evening, when I closed it again, every minute would be unpredictable, because I didn't decide. I didn't choose what would happen next. My entire teenage days were in the hands of another human being.

*

Jimmy this, Jimmy that

I call Noggin Kevin now. Noggin didn't really go down well with the ladies, and most of his girlfriends preferred his Christian name.

'Introducing somebody to your mum and dad as Kevin would naturally seem a bit more favourable for potential parental approval, than explaining to them that, yes, my boyfriend is called Noggin because of that obvious birthmark you can see on his head, and yes, that has been his nickname for years because Noggin is a slang word for your head, and yes, my current boyfriend is very mature, that's why he still harbours the nickname that caused him so much grief as a teenager.'

This is almost word for word the diatribe he presented me with one day, after turning up at my door and announcing, 'Noggin has deceased. It's permanently Kevin from now on.'

Of course I respect this, but still call him Noggin if I want to get under his skin. We were always the closest – not just because Specks was never a friend for the future and Jimmy was always going to end up either dead or in jail. There was always an understanding between us; a deep feeling of warmth and contentment every time I tapped on his door or asked him for advice.

He usually surfaces when Jane is out with her friends and I'm on baby duty – which calls for a few beers, and a general chat about football, parenting and the growing social effect things like Facebook and iPhones are having on the next generation. We genuinely do talk about the latter, because I sometimes look at my four year old son and try to imagine what the world will be like for him. Wonder if he'll grow up and meet a Jimmy Stokes, or if he'll be a technologically induced hermit, confined to a virtual life. This worries me more than anything else. That, and the hope he won't succumb to peer pressure enough to ruin his education, like I did.

Of course, it doesn't take us long to start reminiscing about the old days; our time spent with the legendary Jimmy Stokes. We tend to choose a certain event and laugh about it. Go into great detail about how we felt, what we thought would be the outcome, and if we actually realised how dangerous it was at the time. After his last visit, Kevin phoned me on the way home to remind me of the day Jimmy pulled his knife out on Specks and said to him, 'yer either ma mate or ma victim.'

There's a saying I often heard my dad blurt out at Christmas, after he'd had one too many drinks and some uncle was getting on his nerves: it was, 'aye, you can choose your mates, but no your family.' This rule wasn't really valid for Jimmy, because he chose his mates alright, but they never necessarily chose him.

*

Did I secretly enjoy the fortification that was Jimmy Stokes? Did I ever complain about the fact that there seemed to be a tacit understanding among the small population of our streets, that any mate of Jimmy's was not to be crossed?

Truth be told, it's what got me through the day.

Jimmy

1

It is a Sunday. One of those days when the weather has a bit of an attitude problem. Intentionally being noncommittal and mixing an unrecognisable complexion with an intermittent spitting – gentle enough not to spoil a hairstyle, but firm enough to make its presence known.

Specks, Noggin and I are in the primary school, playing a game of *Barry*. The bar is actually a window ledge, which further adds to the excitement and unpredictability of the game, because kicking the ball too high might result in smashing one of the windows. Being the weekend, the only person who would actually care about this is the janitor, but judging by his waddle, I'm not entirely convinced he'd be willing to spoil his Sunday roast for a few shards of glass.

We take this game very seriously. We even have seeds, and I'm currently seed one, having quite brilliantly defeated almost everyone in our year, and then easily pushing Noggin and Specks to one side.

Jimmy doesn't like football though, so when we see him approaching, we'll kick the ball onto the roof and pretend we were just standing about, discussing the dark arts of social decorum.

Noggin is wearing this awful chequered shirt his mum insists he never leaves home without. Thick, with a nice furry inside.

Specks is usually doing something mischievous. Constructing, then reconstructing some plot to steal a car radio, going up town on a bag-snatching adventure or bragging to a first year at school about his latest trick: the ice-cream van snatch and grab job.

Today, however, there's nothing particularly criminal coming out his mouth, because he's attempting to start a war in the insect kingdom. In one hand he's holding a daddy-long-legs, and in the other a spider – both equal in size, only one with a firmer body, and the other with longer legs. He's talking to them, discussing one another's physical attributes, and who should be more afraid once he's thrown them in the pit: the pit being a small cardboard box that he found lying about the playground.

We all enjoy a certain sense of freedom when Jimmy isn't around: none more so than Specks. He seems to stand to attention – both physically and metaphorically – as soon as the man himself arrives. It's quite an incredible transformation from lion to mouse, tiger to rabbit.

I've got the ball balanced on this cone, and I'm about to attempt what we refer to as the *rugby punt*. This bonus round can only commence if a player hits the bar twice in a row – which I have just quite dazzlingly achieved.

The elevation is because you're attempting to hit the ledge on the second floor of the school. Achieving this means you automatically win the game, so I'm currently focusing on the importance of the task at hand – all the time

Jimmy

trying to shut out Specks' morally corruptive conversation with his two gladiators.

I take a few steps back, and stand tall; preparing my run-up and meticulously judging exactly how many paces I need to gather optimum speed. I look up to the heavens – a perfect parody of a footballer taking a penalty in the World Cup Final – then allow a small glance at Specks, just to ensure he hasn't got bored of his plans, before dropping my gaze back onto the ball; studying it intently, intimately, trying to telepathically send victorious energy towards it. It's one of those balls that have been signed by Roberto Baggio, the magician from Italy, and although we aren't stupid enough to actually believe in the authenticity of the signature, it's still nice to feel like a professional.

I run towards the ball, picking up pace, picturing myself lifting the World Cup, and then WHOOSH! I swing my leg through mid-air and connect with nothing; burling around like a ballerina, fighting with the dust particles floating about the atmosphere and landing painfully on my buttocks. I'm desperate to reach and sooth my behind, but instead find myself looking up, because the ball is travelling higher and higher, reaching for the stars. A feeling of perplexity overcomes me, for I am positive I didn't connect with the leather material and wondering how it can possibly be moving in its current trajectory.

A hidden camera inside the orbit-bound object would enjoy a panoramic view of the following: Specks crushing his little box; me quickly jumping to my feet and wiping the mess from my back side; and Noggin watching the ball, silently praying his kick was hard enough to land on the roof and stay there. This can only mean one thing: Jimmy has just walked round the corner.

He's gesticulating away and spraying words that usually cause the television to go BEEP – carrying a strange looking sports bag, which one: is very unlikely to contain Barbie dolls, and two: most probably doesn't belong to him.

Jimmy has a plan. Barbaric Jimmy, that's what we called him. Not to his face obviously, even though he wouldn't know what the word meant. We learnt that word in History from Mr Griffiths. We very cruelly referred to him as mongo Griff, because he walked funny. Teenagers like to pick up on any imperfection: any opportunity to remind you of your inferior place in society. Griff always referred to Hitler as barbaric. I thought he meant something about a barber shop, referring to his moustache, but after hearing about what he did to the Jews, I came to the conclusion that barbaric was a fitting name for the horrible bastard.

Comparing Jimmy Stokes to Hitler was doing a great disservice to the Nazi rebellion, but there you have it: barbaric Jimmy; the Nazi rebellion.

Jimmy's dad was inside again: three years for something he was obviously innocent of. Naturally, Jimmy was seething. He kept talking about a guy called Peebo. I'd be very surprised if Peebo was even remotely close to his Christian name. It was probably something like George. Take Noggin as an example; the name Noggin is about as close to Kevin as we are to the moon, proving that nicknames are very rarely an abbreviation of your first name, but in fact, usually a permanent reference to some biological malfunction or personality disorder.

Jimmy said Peebo had grassed his dad up, and that stabbing your mates in the back was the ultimate sin. He went on to say that he knew where the guy lived.

It was at this point in the story I started to wish I'd never been born.

The contents of the bag were then disclosed, and just as I imagined, these were not daisies and chrysanthemums. First of all he pulled out a kitchen knife, which he slid in his sleeve. Then he pulled out a dirty baseball bat, and handed it to me. Noggin was given a small metal pole, similar to that of a police officer's truncheon, and Specks was armed with two glass bottles. Throwing the bag on the ground and spitting on it – confirming my suspicion that he wasn't the proprietor, barbaric Jimmy then opened his mouth.

'We're gonnae git this cunt,' he shouts. 'Naebody grasses oan ma fuckin old man.'

Of course, the 'we're' part wasn't a question: it was an order.

*

The clock rests on the wall; alone, conspicuous, and bored with its duty of reminding us how predictable life is. A flicker of the eye from left to right would reveal nothing but white wallpaper, decorated by sporadic flowers and the odd mark of chocolate smeared across it by a child still searching for his place in the world. It is, basically, the least unmaterialistic wall in the universe.

The hands of the clock light up in the dark, and currently read 3.05am. The noises of the nocturnal world float by; taxi doors closing, arguments escalating, drunkards singing out of tune, all beautifully supplemented by the shouting of a four year old coming through the wall.

I glance at Jane, whose sound asleep: breathing in and out with a consistency that most people would envy.

We've put in place what we appositely categorized as *the work arrangement*. It's relatively simple; if Jane's working and I'm not, and Luke wakes up in the middle of the night, I have to get up and attend to him…and vice versa. Having a child is difficult, but we both firmly believe working as a collective unit is what has kept the relationship strong; taking circumstances into account, and being empathetic to the other person's needs; not prioritising either career or thinking one should take on more responsibility than the other.

Jane works as a florist's assistant. She really loves what she does – especially on Valentine's Day when she gets to read all the pathetically sentimental and cringingly romantic notes.

Tomorrow – or today, depending how you look at it – Jane is starting really early, because they have a commission for a wedding.

I work as a customer relations officer for Scottish Hydro. The very sentence makes me want to kill myself. I visit our competitor's customers at home, and exhaust them with a scripted and hugely patronising speech about how much money they can save by moving to Scottish Hydro. Yes, that's about as exciting as it gets. Hardly my idea of paradise, but what is this utopia that everyone talks about anyway? Does it even exist?

A few seconds of sleep-deprived stupefaction pass, before something about a monster is heard from the other room, and Jane sleepily places her hand on my leg – giving it a friendly but meaningful push.

I get up from the bed and go through to check on Luke. Being free from the burden of life must be both wonderful and frightening, but he seems to take everything in his stride.

As I enter the room, Luke shouts, 'the monster is stealing my cars.'

To which I reply, 'that seems like quite an unreasonable monster, pal.'

As I squat down closer to him, I notice his eyes are still closed, but my presence seems to have stirred him a little, opening them a fraction. He doesn't say anything though, just looks at me and smiles. It doesn't matter the pain and anguish a child can put you through; the sleepless nights, the loss of identity, the changes in your marriage, or the permanent loss of your freedom…all of this dissolves with a simple smile.

I rub my hand through his hair, watching his eyelids open and close, and whilst mumbling something encouraging and soporific into the air above his head, I notice the curtain is fractionally open at one side, and a glimmer of night light is coming into the room. After successfully getting him back into his dream world of fire engines and cars, I get up to close the curtain. However, as I approach it, something catches my eye: scaffolding across the road, empty from the day before, ready to be walked across and further used as a support for whatever reconstruction is currently under way. This is only part of what catches my attention, because there's a large teddy in someone's window with its eyes fixed on mine. Mixed in with the street lights and the way it leans to one side, it could almost be standing on the scaffolding, looking down at the world.

We caught this little snobby fucker from another school lurking in territory out with his jurisdiction. When I say 'we', I mean Jimmy. Still wearing his uniform from Stuart Melville College: what was he thinking? Or more to the point, what was he doing here? Did he not realise people from our area hate the middle classes?

Jimmy made him climb up to the top of a scaffolding. Naturally the boy was terrified; not just because the impending threat was to cut off his balls if he didn't do it, but because the scaffolding was three floors high.

Jimmy climbed up after him and grabbed the boy by the hair, shouting all sorts of profanities into his ear. I'm looking at this terrified teenager; his fear, his tears, his pleads for liberation…all mixed in with the obvious realisation that this provocation has no chance whatsoever of ending well for him, and I mutter to myself, 'what a state eh affairs tae git yersell in, ya stupid prick.'

Jimmy climbs back down – not before slapping him in the face – and starts giving us instructions about how we should proceed: first an introductory stage of targeting him with stones. Three shots each. Noggin and I intentionally miss with all three of our efforts – two of them very close though, just to ensure it didn't look like we had any sympathy whatsoever for this out-of-place straggler.

Specks hit him on the shoulder, and then on the leg, before Jimmy perilously connected with his torso, unleashing an onslaught of abuse about being posh and privileged, and how it's 'dinnae and winnae' and not 'don't and won't'.

A bit harsh, to be honest. This boy's articulation was perfectly acceptable.

Lastly, we moved onto the dénouement: the Olympic jump.

Jimmy's shouting and swearing, telling him he better jump, if he knows what's good for him. Specks is laughing, Noggin is looking about for the police, and I'm incredulously staring at Jimmy, praying he's just having a laugh, when suddenly we hear a thud about two metres away from us.

Naturally, this idiot's writhing about the floor, holding one of his ankles, screaming for help.

Jimmy approaches him, and all that remains is a distant muttering and whimpering; Jimmy won't even allow him to enjoy his pain. The boy might be pleading for mercy, but, unfortunately for him, his obviously broken ankle isn't enough to satisfy Jimmy's hunger for barbarity, and he quickly pulls out his knife.

Which is when Noggin steps forward and says, 'surely that's enough!'

There's a short, poignant silence, before Jimmy turns. 'What did ye fuckin say? Ye fancy um or sumthin?'

My reverence for Noggin that day was almost as palpable as my sigh of relief, but actually it should have been the fat boy from the other school thanking him. He didn't, though; he just lay there, looking about, hoping someone would come to his aid.

Jimmy this, Jimmy that

I close the curtain on Jimmy's victim and glance over at Luke. Still fast asleep, so I tip-toe through to the kitchen. Slugging on some fresh mango juice, I don't feel tired in the slightest. Actually, I feel very energetic. The memory from the past has put my mind into overdrive, and instead of trying to stay in back-to-bed mode, I'm thinking about the day ahead, and all the things to be done; one of them being clear out the storage cupboard, because Jane is getting tired of visitors looking at her pants on the clothes horse, and wants to use it as a drying room.

That storage cupboard is littered with superfluous paraphernalia, but one particular item stands out from the rest, exuding a completely different type of memory; not a particular event, but something far weightier. There's nothing joyful about it.

It's the middle of the night, and nobody should be searching for memories in the darkness, but I know exactly which box it went into. I rummage about at the bottom and extract the baseball bat I was given on the eve of Jimmy's barbaric plan. Just as I'm sliding my finger along the bumps in the wood, a creaking is heard from outside the cupboard door. Luke must be up.

I hold the bat behind my back, and force my head round the corner of the door, trying to ascertain if he's just shouting in his sleep again, or actually needs my attention, when I notice Jane standing at the bathroom door.

'What's all the noise about?' she whispers.
'Sorry, I was just looking for something,' I reply.
'You'll wake Luke.'
'I won't…I promise….I'll just be a minute.'

I remember then that Jane bought some of that hot chocolate I really like, so proceed back into the kitchen.

There's a mirror in the hallway, and I look into it, all the time holding the baseball bat firmly in my grip. I look at this person staring back at me; this family man, the perfect picture of responsibility; loving husband, caring father, respectable enough income, generally conscientious.

In amongst this reflection, a young man appears.

I look away from the mirror, down at the bat. Was it just us?

Barbarity was everywhere back then.

2

After handing us the weapons, Jimmy had looked up to the sky, pausing in motion for what felt like forever. We thought he was possibly calling on Zeus, or some other indignant entity residing in the sky, but he was actually looking at the ball. The magnitude of what it had just overheard had obviously affected its stillness, and suddenly it began to shake, and then to fall from the guttering. Jimmy's eyes followed it towards the ground…bounce, bounce, bounce…BANG!

'What did A say aboot fuckin fitbaw!?' Jimmy slowly released his knife from the innards of the ball.

Peebo's house is situated in a high-rise block of flats, a fact Jimmy had apparently acquired from some idiot who had previous with Peebo. Seemed to be the ubiquitous sentence in our area: 'Aye, A've goat previous wi that cunt' – never going into detail, of course.

Before night, Jimmy wanted to do some reconnaissance work, just to ensure we had the right address.

Specks rang the buzzer, but no one answered. We suspected this was because Peebo followed some sort of dealers' code. Then Specks was told to throw a stone at the window. In terms of recon work, this wasn't exactly

Jimmy

the MI5, but our mission for the moment was just to avoid the possibility of getting the wrong person.

Noggin isn't really paying attention. He's smacking the heads off thistles and then volleying them into oblivion, when they present themselves at the optimum height. Noggin hasn't been himself recently. He's been a lot more reticent and surprisingly indifferent to Jimmy's behaviour. This isn't something I enjoy seeing, and I find myself wondering if it has anything to do with the family problem I witnessed a couple of days ago.

'Tiny goat raped last night,' he had told me in his bedroom, a police car still outside on the kerb.

I'm standing there thinking about why he even bothered to let me in in the first place, when I feel a tug on my arm and Jimmy is muttering something like, 'what the fucks up wi you?' into my ear.

At least I think it was that. It certainly wasn't, 'can you please fetch me a one-shot caramel latte.'

I look past Jimmy, fully acknowledging that I've failed to comprehend his remark, because a window has just opened, and two of the angriest people I've ever witnessed are gawping out at us.

*

Cramond harbour: joggers, cappuccino's, and extravagantly named yachts swaying in the water. Enough to make anyone believe they were in Venice. The Western European feeling is further backed-up by a warm breeze – meaning

Jimmy this, Jimmy that

the general population are bereft of overcoats and scarves: an anomaly for Edinburgh.

Jane is holding Luke by the hand and pointing to a little coffee shop that looks onto the water.

Luke has a short attention span, so when the waitress comes over, Jane quickly orders a double espresso, a latte for herself, and a small apple juice – haughtily asking about the nature of the child's glass and whether it will come with a straw.

The waitress jots down our order, and then glances at me and winks, before making her way to another table. Steady on – was she flirting with me there? Jane is too busy tickling Luke to notice, but surely it was just wishful thinking that this young woman would be interested in a married man marred by four years of sleep deprivation.

Jane told me this morning that she wanted to talk to me. Something serious. Probably something about Luke. Maybe I've not been taking potting training seriously enough.

I get up to pay, wanting to test my theory about the waitress. Monika; a nice European name; short blond hair, a petite figure, and a delicately poised countenance. She glances at me and says, 'how did your son enjoy his apple juice?'

'I think he preferred the waitress,' I reply, returning her wink.

She blushes, shyly giggles and then retorts in a husky whisper, 'well, he's a handsome little man: takes after his father.'

I knew she thought I was hot.

Afterwards, Jane and I venture along the walkway, me with my hands in my pockets, and Luke scurrying about searching for anything and everything. Jane sighs as if to say, 'don't worry, I'll run after him all day.'

She's right, I'm being very presumptuous.

'Did you ask your mum about next week?' I say, trying to conjure up a civil conversation.

'Not yet,' she answers, running after Luke, who has spotted a puppy on the other side of the walkway.

This is what most of our conversations are like now that we have a child: lacking in flow, which I find hurtful, but try not to comment on.

I've always been a bit of a thinker; someone who is only actually present part of the day – spending the rest of the time in a world of my own, over-analysing every aspect of my existence. Jane said I'm a bit like her dad, which was the initial attraction.

As I scoop my son up to confirm that I'm not going to leave all the parenting to Jane, I get to thinking about something my mum asked me yesterday.

'Difficult not having her undivided attention anymore?' she had said, in that sentimental but inquisitive tone a mother employs when she's prying about your current emotional state of affairs.

We arrive at the waterfall and Jane decides to put on Luke's reigns. This is understandable, because although there's a barrier – which is supposed to protect people from falling over the edge – it doesn't look like the council have commissioned anyone to fix it for about a hundred years.

Having ignored all signs of danger, four teenage boys are lingering about the waterfall in a perfect parody of

Jimmy this, Jimmy that

my youth. One of them is standing laughing at another boy struggling to swim, awkwardly doing the front crawl towards safe land. This would no doubt have been Specks. The other two are standing in disgust, wondering if they will get in trouble for helping their friend who could drown: this would be Noggin and I, forever the middle-men. Looking at the king standing on his mountain, staring down and laughing at his victim, it becomes obviously evident that the victim was told to jump, and having refused, was pushed. A certain part of me is desperate to shout and ask if the tormentor's name happens to be Jimmy, when I hear a voice behind me saying, 'so, it's probably a good thing we didn't throw it out, then.'

I turn and look at Jane, who is holding our child firmly in her arms, and staring at me with intent. She has that glaze in her eyes, like she's just told me something important that could either make or break us. However, I wasn't actually listening, because I was lost in the world of Jimmy again. Wait, is this the moment?

'Did you even listen to a word I just said?'

'Ye…ye, I did. You said…eh… it's good we didn't throw it out.'

'I'm pregnant again,' she says softly.

A pause, and then another pause, before something foggy materialises right in front of my eyes. A cloud of fear and incomprehensible movements, before I say, 'is that what you wanted to – '

'Yes…I thought the waterfall was beautiful and…' she pauses, and then looks past me, staring into the surrounding trees.

'Great…that's great,' I mumble.

'Is it?' she says, a tear starting to roll down her cheek.

'Ye...Jane, why are you crying? Come here.' I take her in my arms.

This is the last thing I expected her to talk to me about. It's obviously come as a big surprise to her, and I know she wanted to manage the new store, which obviously won't happen now. I'm terrified that her tears were because she thinks I hate being a parent, or that I'll try and convince her one is enough. Then I pull away from her and take Luke into my arms. 'Well...fuck me.'

I've managed to calm the situation slightly by bringing humour into it, but she still manages to ask me the ultimate question. 'Are you ok about this?'

I could choose to go off on one about the early stages, the money problems, the fact I was enjoying the three hours a day Luke was at nursery, and how I don't particularly want to raise another child, because I feel as though this one has ripped my soul apart and crushed my identity... but I decide to take the empathetic approach. The approach of the supportive husband who recognises that this could mean another nine months of unpredictability for Jane – not to mention the barbaric labour at the end of it, and quietly reply, 'are you?'

In a strange but slightly perverse way of trying to assuage the situation, she says, 'saw you flirting with that waitress.'

'That was just a bit of – '

'I'm not accusing you of anything. I just...don't want you to feel trapped.'

I look into the rushing tide and the victim is gone. I look to the top of the waterfall and the Jimmy wannabe has disappeared. I look back to Jane and say, 'if it's twins, I want a divorce.'

She laughs. Wipes her face with the sleeve of her jacket.

'Come on,' She says. 'I could do with another coffee.'

3

Although the four of us carried around a certain collective eminence, we couldn't escape from the horrible reality that we were still in school, lingering in the primitive stages of the teenage years. This being the case, we couldn't yet boast of the comforts older people take for granted; their own house, with their own rules of engagement; not having to stand in front of a mirthful class, reading some indecipherable passage from Joseph Conrad's *Heart of Darkness*, constantly being patronised by a teacher who looks like a fucking goat; the luxury of being able to walk into a shop and buy alcohol without wearing your big cousin's jacket, or pointlessly combing your hair into a side-parting; and finally, the seemingly trivial but hugely significant moment when the metaphorical banner hanging from your shoulders that quite embarrassing reads *Young Team*, eventually falls to the ground, being replaced by a whole plethora of items that unequivocally confirm your place as an *adult*.

So when these two people stared down at us from five floors up, it instantly struck me as not only befitting regarding their position in life, but a brutally honest assessment of ours.

They looked similar in appearance; skinheads, tattoos, and a physique that spoke of months behind bars lifting weights. However, the disparity in the consistency of their visits to the dentist was clear, and something told me the one with the rotting dentures was most likely Peebo. I only truly recognised the extremity of this problem, when he opened his mouth and shouted, 'Who the fuck are you?'

This singular enquiry being aimed at Jimmy alone, because he had slightly moved forward, making it obvious he was the antagonist, and we were just his physical and moral support – if we actually looked convincing enough to be classed as either.

Jimmy retorted the following:

'A'm fuckin Jimmy Stokes. Who the fuck are you?'

To which Peebo's friend replied, 'Davie's laddie? Why did ye no say?'

I could tell this unexpectedly cordial answer had slightly thrown Jimmy, because for a moment he sort of looked to the side, reticent. Then he shouted, 'which one eh you pricks is Peebo?'

There seemed to be a moment of nothingness, whilst Peebo and his friend took this in and Jimmy evidently searched for his next line of assault.

'Did you just call me a prick?' Peebo says, fractionally muffled, probably because his associate had just handed him a joint, which he couldn't wait to put in his mouth.

His friend then starts laughing and blurts out, 'Yer aboot fourteen, mate – '

Obviously insulted by the mocking of the one aspect of his life he can't directly effect, Jimmy starts hurling a barrage of abuse; calling Peebo a 'grass,' his mate a 'poofter,' and then saying he's 'coming back later wi his troops tae kick fuck oot eh thum.'

How very prudent of Jimmy to reveal his future plan of assault.

The friend of Peebo's – obviously the joker of the two – glances at us, laughs, and says, 'ye gonnae bring the headmaster anaw?'

Never one for admitting defeat, and ensuring he gets the last word, Jimmy retorts with a rather jovial, 'we'll see…' before turning his back on them and looking at us rather menacingly.

In no time at all though, Jimmy, getting nothing from us, turns back around in the direction of the skinheads. However, after something about 'bring yer science project,' Peebo decides to close the window, leaving Jimmy staring up at the silhouette of his adversary.

Noggin nudges me and then gives me an enquiring look as if to ask me if I have any idea what Jimmy is going to do next, when it suddenly dawns on me: he's searching for a sizeable enough stone or brick that can be thrown at the window. On finding one, he marches over to Specks and demands him to take aim.

Specks quite dexterously hurls the stone, connecting perfectly with the window in question, and although not smashing it, evidently creating a crack in the top right corner.

Jimmy shouts up something that doesn't merit repetition, before patting Specks on the back of the head.

Did Jimmy just show some *affection*?

And why is Specks smiling and gloating as if approval from Jimmy will win him a Nobel Prize?

Within a matter of seconds, the window is open again, and this time neither Peebo nor his friend look like they're about to say something remotely cordial. In fact, Peebo is holding something seriously threatening in his right hand, and then they disappear.

The closing of the window a second time, and the lack of obvious audible retaliation, would indicate that they're probably on their way down the stairs, so at the signal of Jimmy, we depart.

*

A week or so before Jimmy declared war on the skinheads, the man himself wasn't out. He was away doing a favour for one of his cousins. The nature of this favour was kept under wraps, but I'd be very surprised if it involved doing something altruistic for humanity.

It was a sunny afternoon, and we intended to make the most of every minute of Jimmy's absence; laughing and joking without fear of being judged; enjoying a new card game Noggin had invented called *shithead*, not to mention the bottle of cider Specks had pilfered from his dad's cabinet.

It was *nice*, and nice is not the sort of word I'd normally associate with my youth.

We began in McDonald's. Because being so used to dictation, and not fully comprehending the use of democratic behaviour, Noggin had suggested the best way to proceed would be to make one decision each; and this was his.

Enjoying diversity in our choices, we strolled out satisfied and made our way into Stockbridge because Specks wanted to look around the shops.

Jimmy

As we approached the main street of this predominantly middle-class part of Edinburgh, I could sense a slight nervousness emanating from Noggin, and although I wasn't a mind reader, I knew exactly what he was thinking, when he fleetingly glanced at me, because I had wondered about it myself. Specks being a kleptomaniac, 'Lit's have a look roond the shoaps,' wasn't really his idea of fun, unless he had something more sinister up his sleeve. We two, however, were of the understanding that any day without Jimmy was to be free from barbarity and transgression.

Of course the real dilemma – which would crop up time and time again, even though Noggin had attempted some sort of mutual understanding – was that without Jimmy, there wasn't really a natural leader. Noggin was obviously the most intelligent and me probably the best fighter, but Specks exuded a different type of personality: someone you'd never really respect, but would always be cautious of. Aside from all this, added to his sentence was, 'A need tae get a present fur ma mum.' A present she so obviously deserved.

The problem certainly wasn't any feeling of allegiance towards the shop owner, for although in later life I would come to realise that people are just people, at this stage in my evolution I was of the opinion that being from an area like Stockbridge meant you were a snobby bastard, and you deserved everything you got.

In the end I decided to ignore Noggin's fleeting glance, instead surreptitiously encouraging Specks to steal from a shop where the counter assistant was more interested in dusting the shelves than catching three youths entering with nothing, and leaving with everything.

For my turn, I had decided on a trip to Inverleith Park. I'd like to say this was to enjoy a gentle stroll around the pond. In reality, it was the thrill I got out of throwing stones at the swans and provoking them into attack. An older woman – dressed like a homeless person and hurling pieces of bread to the ducks – was absolutely furious at us for this, and started screaming about the strength of the swan's bite.

'That's the whole point ya smelly old cow,' shouted Specks. 'It's called a dare.'

The poor woman was just trying to warn us, but never contradict a teenager. It won't end well.

The afternoon concluded with a well-earned seat on the grass, drinking cider and watching the joggers go by, giving the females marks out of ten.

For a short hiatus, it seemed that just being was enough, and a mild contentment surrounded us, sitting there, pretending to be ordinary citizens enjoying a picnic.

*

Kevin is here, and with Luke breathing peacefully underneath his new fireman Sam duvet, we're enjoying a couple of beers and a chinwag. Jane is at her friend's house, attending a surprise get-together for the celebration of her pregnancy.

At the other house, people will be congratulating her, hugging her, passing about little pathetic presents, all mixed in with air kisses and the ritual analysing of the *Names for Kids* handbook. Here, there is the feeling of ambivalence, almost like we're at the wake of a funeral and everyone is saying sorry for your loss. This is slightly augmented because Kevin has just said, 'I thought you were just having one?'

And I've just sardonically replied, 'should have put something on the end of it eh…'

Of course I can afford this type of approach in front of Kevin, because he's my mate, and he understands – having two children of his own. It's all roses and daisies in front of Jane though, and although some people might accuse me of a lack of honesty, I would retort by saying it's merely tactical. Besides, I'm not completely averse to the thought of another child; I'm just ambiguous about it. Why wouldn't I be? I'm only human.

I don't want to dwell on this particular topic for too long, because I hardly get to enjoy his company nowadays, so don't want him going back home thinking I've turned into a miserable old fool who can't handle the thought of an extension to my family.

The entirety of the aforementioned is quite aptly confirmed when Kevin grabs us two beers each and says, 'I brought you two, mate. I thought we might need them.' Then he pauses, before saying, 'forgot to tell you: we've been looking into schools for the wee man. Remember school?'

We then begin to enjoy painting a perfect picture of how brilliant certain aspects of school were. Not the educational side obviously, although we all knew Kevin enjoyed perfect attendance in most of his classes. Intelligent

Jimmy this, Jimmy that

and furtive Noggin: famous for the line, 'Of course A niver studied. Fuck knows how A goat an A plus…'

I envied the guy's ability to find the middle ground. As soon as Jimmy cottoned onto it, he started getting Cs, and then went straight back to the As as soon as Jimmy moved onto something else.

Jimmy was obviously the top boy in our school. That goes without saying. He controlled the fighting, the skiving, the cigarette corner, the canteen; he even occasionally told the teachers what the story was. Jimmy was like the godfather. You had to hand it to him.

He was probably in school a little more than a guy of his ilk was expected to be, so we had to act a certain way depending on his appearance, or lack thereof. However, being in school didn't necessarily guarantee attendance in classes. We would swagger about when he was in, but walk a bit less conspicuously when he didn't turn up.

Strange how the most respected people in society are the ones you'd never invite to your grans for soup. I guess it all comes down to fear, and in high-school fear took precedence over every other emotion. Even had girls coming up to us and simply saying, 'please tell Jimmy I said Hi'. Pathetic really: the guy was just a clown and a bully.

There was actually another reason Kevin had brought up this subject, and it was because he had been trying to remember the reason Jimmy's attendance wasn't actually that bad – even though we all knew there was no longevity in higher education for the Stokes man and we were pretty confident it was only a matter of time before he voluntarily called it a day, was expelled, or arrested for stabbing the headmaster.

Just as Kevin was talking to me about this thought, we both simultaneously shouted out, 'HIS ENTERPRISE', before laughing and almost choking on our beers.

Jimmy ran a cigarette selling business – or *fags* as we called them at school. He called it *His Enterprise*. He most definitely got this name from a gangster movie.

It's very difficult to imagine Jimmy as a successful entrepreneur, but he was actually quite good at it. He even had specific prices for buying individual cigarettes, and offered deals for those buying in bulk.

He certainly walked about the school like he was Gangster number one, and when someone approached what was very aptly named *Jimmy's corner*, he would start off by saying, 'Are ye here tae complete a transaction?'

He even exuded a far calmer countenance: that of a business man trying to please the customer. I think he even said thank you to his buyers.

Problem came when Jimmy was forced to employ a few members of staff. Whether he paid them a salary or not was very debatable. It might have come as a pleasant surprise that he didn't ask us, but we decided it was probably because he wanted people to think we were actually his friends.

After Jimmy was expelled, a girl in Geography told me that Simon Crofter had grassed him up to the head. Simon happened to be one of the employees Jimmy had bullied into helping him, and apparently his mum had found a hundred cigarettes in his school bag with a list of transactions. Threatened to ground him for life if he never told her everything.

Jimmy this, Jimmy that

So Jimmy started running his business outside of the school, but it wasn't very successful for the following reasons. He couldn't gain access into the grounds, therefore couldn't bully anyone into helping him. His chosen spot for business was in a damaged set of bushes just before you enter Inverleith Park, meaning to acquire cigarettes you also had to skip your next class. Finally, he had started selling weed for one of his cousins and so was seen as a very dangerous person to be acquainted with, considering at any given time he could be carrying an ounce of opium laced marijuana.

In the end, he did try and bully us into being his employees on the inside. However, after collectively agreeing to ensure very low sales right from the off, Jimmy eventually lost hope and moved on.

And I don't mean intellectually or spiritually.

4

When I got home that afternoon, baseball bat half tucked into my trousers and half tucked into my t-shirt, and my mum said, 'hi pal, how was your day?,' my response was to ignore her altogether, swiftly moving through the hallway, entering my room and depositing the baseball bat under my bed.

Of course, she could have demanded attention by choosing a particular aspect of my life that to completely ignore would be deemed highly rude and completely insensitive, like: 'how is Noggin's sister, I heard she got raped?'

How would I answer that? 'Aye, mum, she did, and kin ye stoap talkin tae yer fourteen year old son aboot rape, cos it's makin eez feel a bit awkward.'

Luckily, my mum's well aware I'm at a stage in my evolution where most things are a secret, and everything about adults is embarrassing.

The middle of the teenage years might just be the most difficult of your life.

*

Jimmy this, Jimmy that

Jake sways back and forward, scrutinising the world around him and softly muttering a disgruntled soliloquy about it being his 53rd birthday, and how his wife is a complete bitch. He has all the facial attributes of an alcoholic; dry skin, saliva from both corners of the mouth; haggard eyes. Jake is the local drunkard, who can usually be located standing outside the shops asking people for money for another can of super-tennents. His current choice of drink is a large plastic bottle – presumably white lightning, merry-down, or one of the other cheap brands of Cider. Apt that his name is Jake, because *Jakey Bastard* is the saying we use for people of his ilk.

We're currently in the midst of a game that involves money, so it's surely only a matter of time before he approaches us.

We're playing *pitchy* – with a high kerb as the chosen target. The rules of the game are simple: all players throw their coin – usually a 50p or pound, because they're the highest denomination available and to suggest anything less would be showing a sign of weakness – attempting to get it as close to the target as possible. Whoever gets closest then picks up all the coins, throws them in the air, and shouts heads or tails. When they land, all coins falling on the side you chose, you keep. If all of them do, you keep them all: this is called a *full scoop*.

We play this at school with about ten or fifteen people, so a full scoop is almost impossible. However, today it's just the four of us, so it could quite easily happen. If it doesn't though, the person whose coin landed second closest will then have a chance to toss up the remaining coins and attempt to guess what side they will fall on…and so on and so on. Basically, the closer you get to the wall, the better chance you have of winning the most money.

I remember one lunch time, Barry Davidson got a full scoop in an eleven person game, and Jimmy was furious because he claimed a hole in the ground diverted his coin in the wrong direction. Barry told him to stop being a bad loser, and eventually they got into a fight. No prizes for guessing who came out on top. Pitchy at school stopped for a while after this, because people didn't fancy having to fight for their winnings. It was only once Jimmy was expelled for his *Enterprise* that it picked up again.

We play it all the time outside of school, though, and surprisingly enough, Jimmy seems to take defeat quite graciously. Might be something to do with the fact that we usually allow him to win.

Today, Jimmy wins the first game – fairly, believe it or not – and then just as expected, Jake clocks us and slowly makes his way over to watch.

Confronted with four indifferent teenagers, he starts spitting out something about his daughter being a slag, and how she drinks too much. Whispers in my ear, 'A've missed ye mate.' This regurgitation of utter shite produces a choking laugh from Noggin, who nudges him out the way so he can concentrate on his shot. Jake pulls a rusty 10p from his pocket and asks if he can join in. Jimmy calmly mutters, 'fuck off, Jake, A'm tellin ye.' This would be Jimmy in first gear. Not really upsetting his constitution, but emitting enough horse power to subtly get his point across.

Noggin turns to the muttering Jake, and says, 'mate, time tae move oan.'

'Just looking fur a bit eh company,' Jake replies.

A different group of civilians would probably take into account his loneliness, harmlessness, hardship, and general bad luck in life – gently moving him onto pastures new, or even offering him the chance to join in for one round.

Jimmy, however, viciously grabs him by the neck and quite effortlessly shoves him to the ground – from first gear to fourth, avoiding the natural process of evolution as always.

Specks thinks this is hilarious, because he's about as emotionally intelligent as a carcass.

An intoxicated Jake, probably imagining he's the heavyweight champion of the world but actually looking like a dancing fairy, starts bobbing and weaving in a pugilistic manner.

Jimmy goes over to him again, and after attempting a really slow, awkward punch, Jake falls against Jimmy's chest. For the second time, Jimmy grabs him by the neck, before saying, 'A'm fuckin warnin ye ya stinkin prick.'

Jake finds this funny, so Jimmy smacks him in the mouth, and the drunkard collapses to the floor – bulge instantly beginning to materialise under his left eye.

I can't help feeling the pathos involved in watching this man lying on the concrete, drool coming from his mouth, almost in tears because his bottle of cider has rolled onto a drain and the contents are seeping down it. I think about ways this could have been prevented and come to the conclusion that he made his own bed. His downfall was actually his excessive drinking, and this incident no doubt welcome in a perverse sort of way.

Jimmy

As I grit my teeth together in disgust, because Jake is sucking cider from the ground, cupping it into his hands, I can't help but wonder how often I will be accessory to Jimmy's crimes. If I ever had to stand up in court, I'd say to the judge: 'aye, A wis accessory tae the law eh Jimmy Stokes,' to which he would no doubt reply: 'unfortunately, young man, no such law exists. I wonder if you might be thinking of – ' to which I would stop him and say: 'forgive ma impertinence in a court eh law yer honour, but you have tae trust me. I assure ye such a law does exist.'

'Should we no run?' Noggin is saying.

'Na. Fuck um,' Jimmy retorts. 'Lit's git back tae the game. Naebody gees a fuck aboot um anyway.'

This allows me to further evaluate Jake's position in society and even in my attempt to sympathise with him, at the same time I have to accept the truth behind Jimmy's response: nobody *does* care.

*

Throughout all the emotional turbulence, moments of adolescent release, and a complete lack of morality on Jimmy's part, times were still brilliant. We still managed to have a laugh, because not everything Jimmy did was at the expense of our morals, and to his credit, at least there was nothing fake about him: what you saw was what you got. Always.

One of his favourite practical jokes was to order a Chinese takeaway from the local phone box, and send it to the address across the street. We would hang about outside the stair door, waiting for the guy to arrive with the delivery, and then laughing at him getting irate over the practical joke. He would be shouting things like 'well, who is accountable?' and 'someone has to pay.'

One time – after replacing the phone on the receiver – Jimmy turned to us and said, 'Cunt, they've stoaped deliverin tae this street. How fuckin funny is that?'

There was a girl from our area called Stacey, who had to drop out of school because she got pregnant, and every time she was close by, Jimmy would put his hands up his top and waddle about, muttering some young parent related expletive under his breath.

At the weekends, Jimmy liked to orchestrate the *garden run*. Basically, you had to run through as many gardens as you could without getting caught, or at the very worst getting away with nothing but a threat to phone the police. The game usually came to an abrupt halt when Specks noticed something hanging on a washing line that he thought would look better on his own back. He once stole something from Big Eddie's washing line at the bottom of the street, and ended up locked in a cupboard whilst the big guy decided his fate. Eventually he let him away with a warning because he couldn't be bothered with the hassle. I doubt this was the only reason though; like I said, with Jimmy, it wasn't all bad. He did usually have your back, even if indirectly.

We seemed to spend a lot of time on roofs; sports centres, schools, and the occasional house that the council were in the process of constructing. Something about the height, the danger, the looking down on the world passing by that seemed to elate us. We enjoyed smoking cigarettes, pissing off the edge – hoping the wind didn't blow it back in our faces – and throwing stones at buses, cars, Lorries. Specks once caused a crash, which Jimmy thought was hilarious.

The roof of the sports centre was shaped like an arc, and in the winter we would slide from the top and jam our feet into the gutter at the edge. Considering the roof was relatively icy at this time of year, this was a fatal accident waiting to happen. Mind you, every day with Jimmy was a near-death experience.

I'm not sure what the people in the sports hall thought about all the noise. The caretaker sometimes came out, but after Jimmy told him to 'fuck off' several times, and he replied he didn't get paid enough to deal with this kind of nonsense, we usually continued our game with impunity. I often wondered why he didn't just phone the police. Maybe he didn't want the neighbours to think he couldn't deal with us. The fact that we were there all the time meant he obviously couldn't.

On bank holidays – or just days that he decided to skive school – Specks would usually venture out to Clermiston or Corstorphine for a steal: or a *chorey* as he called it.

These trips were always premeditated, and the night before would usually end with him saying, 'Fuck school, A'm gawn up clery fur a chore the morn. Youse up fur it?'

Noggin and I would then strive to ensure the subject was quickly changed, so Specks had no ammunition to further press the issue...or worse, Jimmy got on board.

He usually abstained from shops in our area – however, on one occasion he tried his luck in the local corner shop.

This was a stupid thing to do, because not only did he sell us cigarettes at fourteen, he was known to turn a blind eye to people of sixteen purchasing a bottle of vodka.

After a serious confrontation involving Specks, the owner, and obviously Jimmy – who wouldn't miss out on something like this – the shop door was closed. With a mixture of resentment that we probably couldn't enter the only shop that sold us cigarettes again, and happiness that the encounter had come to a close, Noggin and I began to make our way down the street. It only took us a few steps to realise that the other two hadn't followed; in fact, it only took us another few steps to hear the smashing sound. Jimmy had decided to put a brick through the guy's window. Ironic really, considering it wasn't even Jimmy's battle to fight, however, you could tell that Specks was delighted someone of Jimmy's eminence was sticking up for him. We probably should have run down the street at this point, but then we would have had to endure Jimmy's wrath at a later date, for being cowards. So we decided to go back up the road. When we got there, through the smashed glass I could see the owner on the phone to the police. Jimmy instantly turned to me and said, 'A've goat a fuckin great idea. Specks, git roond tae that other shoap and git us some eggs. Dinnae steal thum, though, ya daft cunt.'

This is what ensued: Jimmy phoned the police and said that, 'aye, eh wis guilty, but if they even considered tryin tae dae anythin aboot it, they would aw die.'

As soon as he hung up, I turned my attention to Specks approaching us waving a big box of eggs. Was this really Jimmy's interpretation of a great idea?

Jimmy

Picture the scene: bushes, four teenagers holding three eggs each; a police car slowly approaching, driver looking from left to right; Jimmy Stokes muttering, 'ready, ready, ready, GO!' The aforementioned four people – all equally important enough to be called the protagonist in this particular story – moving from behind the bush, and throwing eggs in the direction of the car; laughing, shouting, swearing and congratulating each other on any contact of egg yolk on the antagonist's vehicle. The police car then screeches to a halt and the driver gets out – pointing at us, saying something under his breath and then talking into his radio. On noticing the villains turn and run, the assailant jumps back into his car and puts his foot down.

Tears of joy and laughter rolling down our cheeks, we had absolute confidence in our escape – knowing this area better than anyone.

In the end they went back to the station as failures: two police officers unable to enforce the law on four jubilant teenagers.

*

The electrician is here. He's fitting two spotlights in the kitchen that Jane so enthusiastically purchased from Ikea yesterday.

I'm sitting on the couch reading through a pamphlet we were given at the nursery, grumbling that I thought the whole point of nursery was to help them learn the basic principles of social decorum, and not expect them to already know it. Jane's always telling me these things are just arbitrary and I shouldn't take everything as some sort of personal injustice. I'm thinking about how she's probably right when I notice the word TINY written in capital letters, and suddenly start thinking about the next time I went to Noggin's house.

Of course there wasn't a huge amount of conversation between Tiny and me anyway, but even if there was, what do you say to a victim of rape; 'how you doing?' Isn't it obvious! 'How was the sex?' Are you actually fucking joking! 'och, it'll be ok.' Will it? Will it really?

I guess this is probably why I stopped going to his house: I just couldn't deal with it. When I told Noggin I'd just start meeting him at the corner with Specks, he didn't say anything, but I could tell he knew. Was this a betrayal? At fourteen does it really matter?

She was always just *Tiny* to me: Noggin's sister. However, now she was *raped Tiny*: Noggin's unfortunate sister.

My memory is broken by loud laughter coming from the kitchen, so I get up to check out what's going on. The electrician has doubled over and Jane has her hand on his shoulder, simultaneously wiping a tear from her eye with the sleeve of her other hand. I uncomfortably chuckle, just to let them know I'm watching, then cross my arms as if to say, 'caught ya!'

Jane turns round to face me and says, 'Luke just...'

'Uh huh,' I reply.

I glance at her hand, then at the electricians shoulder, and then she glances at her hand, and then turns and looks at the area it was just so suspiciously placed. On turning back to look into my eyes, I can read exactly what she's thinking – 'how dare you accuse me of flirting with this man, considering how many times you've dropped at the feet of sixteen year old waitresses and every other female on the planet who has two legs and two tits.'

Of course she doesn't say any of this.

After the electrician leaves and Jane stands turning the lights on and off for what feels like about an hour, she comes to sit down beside me on the couch.

'All sorted,' I mutter in a placatory manner.

She doesn't answer.

'Where's Luke?' I say.

'He's sleeping in our bed,' she replies. She has an intensity about her. Not the jubilant new owner of kitchen spotlights, but the bearer of bad news. 'Things will have to change again…for a while.'

'Great,' I say, praying it sounded more supportive than resentful.

'You might have to do a few more hours at work.'

'That's ok, I love my job.'

Shouldn't couples be having sex whilst their child is sleeping?

'I didn't know you played baseball,' she says.

'I didn't.'

'But you've got a bat in the cupboard?'

There's a stirring panic inside my head. 'You'd better not throw that out!'

'There was me thinking I was the one with hormone problems! Fine, we'll keep it…'

'Thank you.' I lift up her jumper and softly caress her protruding stomach. 'I hope it's a boy.'

'Why!?' she spurts out, defensively.

I pull down her jumper and slowly sit up. I kiss her on the cheek and then jump to my feet.

'Because, soon to be mother of two screaming children... I've already decided what I think we should call him.'

5

Until you're involved in something, faced with the fear of it, you'll never know how you'd respond.

Imagine for a moment the ramifications if we let Jimmy down. This wouldn't be business or even family. This would be honour, integrity and trust.

We know our friendship with Jimmy is as strong as melting ice.

If we suddenly disappeared from Jimmy's life, there'd be no mourning period; he would simply move on and use someone else. Trouble is, he decides when our time is up.

Everyone needs guidance from above: a councillor of some sort; a therapist to help you discover your more spiritual side. This is Jimmy's role. He's our spiritual guide. The only difference is, unlike a professional, Jimmy's nature of working is unorthodox: he's searching for the spiritual side that would land us outside the front door of Satan. We'd knock…and knock… and then the devil himself would answer, saying, 'you want to talk about choices…let's talk about choices.'

How I've managed to stay awake is a mystery. I suppose adrenaline mixed in with fear isn't exactly a brilliant combination for overcoming temporary insomnia.

Jimmy this, Jimmy that

I feel for Noggin. The police have just been at his door about his little sister. The last thing his parents need is another visit from the old bill to say their other child was involved in a homicide.

If that's what Jimmy has planned.

I've actually grown tired of asking myself the question about what the future holds. I've gone over and over it and the final outcome always seems dark. It would have been far more enjoyable to sit in my bed thinking about Tracey Anderson – the hottest girl in our school – instead of trying to predict the order of proceedings; what happens when we get to the door? Do we just walk in? It's not like we're dealing with an old age pensioner. What if we all die? Don't think I haven't thought about this: about how life is defined by a single choice.

During this three or four hour period when I was supposed to be sleeping, but was actually trying to predict the future, I suddenly became someone else; a philosopher, a practitioner, a person of great knowledge.

They say on the verge of death your life flashes before your eyes. Maybe I should start organising the pictures, just to ensure they capture the best moments?

But forget about my death. What if I'm forced to attack? What if I do attack? What if I become a murderer? What if Peebo ends up in the afterlife and I'm incarcerated in some correctional facility for the under aged.

I even contemplate prayer – trying to remember some of the nonsense our R.E teacher said to us about absolution, forgiveness and sanctity.

I think about the movie I watched at Noggins, where the guy is on death row. All the inmates would wait for

Monday morning: the 'day of execution'. The execution officer would slowly walk along the corridor and from every cell would come a sigh of relief: a moment of recognition that this wasn't their time. Their life would go on for a little longer: at least another week. I tried to remember the words of the protagonist the day he was chosen to make the walk. When they stopped at his cell, he looked up from his bed and said: 'today is my birthday. The day I was born is the day I will die.'

I step off the bed and stand for a second: taking in the world around me. I hear the distant snoring of my dad and mice in places they're never welcome; gnawing and scraping in a perfect parody of my insides. I open the curtains and look at the murky skyline.

I retrieve the baseball bat from under the bed, before slowly opening my bedroom door, just to check for any signs of life, closing it again and breathing in. Everything is in place.

*

We loved it when Jimmy met a bird. Sometimes he'd sneak away to some unoccupied alleyway and come back with a grin on his face: the post-orgasm inner smile, winking and saying the same quote all the time, 'ye ken me boys. Niver one tae turn doon a ride.' Then he'd ruin our moment of sexual envy by saying something derogatory to Specks, like, 'Nixt time A'l borrow yer glasses.'

I suppose the thing about Jimmy and females was he fitted the profile perfectly. It might not have made much sense to us, but when you take into account his arrogance, his sexual experience for a guy of only fourteen, the fact that he was a top boy – not looking for commitment – I suppose you could see how all these contributing factors would give him a certain sexual allure. Later in life none of these girls would give a guy like Jimmy a second glance, but when you're a teenager, kids, houses and security aren't even on the horizon, never mind etched into the agenda of current priorities.

On one particularly memorable occasion, Jimmy's post sexual preaching about the particulars of the vagina was instantly interrupted – by him, obviously: we would never speak over him – because he suddenly had a thought, and then pulled out a leaflet from his jacket pocket. His preaching swung from the clitoris to his views about religion. 'This fuckin leaflit came through the door eh, wi fuckin *Jesus loves ye* oan it. Now A ken it wasnae just ma hoose they went tae, but A'm still taking it fuckin personally, and A want us tae go up there and show they cunts they made a big mistake. Fancy a wee trip tae the church boys?'

When the priest greets us with, 'hallo children,' Noggin mutters, 'patronising cunt: A'm fourteen.'

'Eh meant children in the spiritual way,' retorts Specks, provoking an acknowledgement from us that he was successfully getting into the appropriate character, even though all the time he was looking at Jimmy and not us. After all, Jimmy was seeking aided retribution for littering his house with pious leaflets, and Specks wasn't going to let him down.

Sadly Specks' moment of theatrical brilliance went unnoticed by Jimmy, because he was too busy saying, 'cunt, look at this place. A'v always wanted tae ride a bird in a church.'

As the melodic piano playing starts, we take our seats and watch the minister move dreamlike towards the pulpit – nodding to as many regulars as possible and passing his eyes over us deferentially, but not without inquisition.

An older woman plants her rather oversized backside down beside Specks.

'Lovely to see so many young people attending church. This secular attitude nowadays is really upsetting, don't you think?' She then smiles a warm, spiritual, patronising and condescending smile.

'Secular ya cunt. What the fuck's she oan aboot?' says Jimmy.

'A think she said sexular,' I respond.

Jimmy looks a bit confused about this, and just grunts a forced laugh.

Of course this is the moment Specks had been waiting for, and ending her sentence with a question mark is probably the worst thing she could have done. Specks lifts his head, clutching again at the bible, then replies, 'ever since ma grandfather was killed by the Nazi's, A've always looked up tae God as a sort eh grandfather figure. They even share the same facial hair.'

'How lovely,' says the pious old cow. 'Tell me, what do you think is the most important commandment?'

And this was when I knew our first visit to the church would be fleeting, because Specks turned to her and said, 'thou shalt no shite in the church because God doesnae provide toilet paper.'

And as if he had been suppressing it for a number of years, Jimmy explodes; a mixture of laughter, tears, blasphemies, and gesticulations – all aimed in Specks' direction.

Jimmy then adds in, 'ya cunt, does God even wipe his erse?'

This brings a choir like laughter from all of us that seems to go on forever, and then the older woman starts crying, crossing herself repetitively and looking over in the direction of the minister – who is trying to ignore this disruption and move forward with proceedings.

The laughter abates and Jimmy says loudly, 'HERE, dae we git tae drink wine at this yin?'

The lady gets up and moves away from us. I watch her talking to someone and pointing at us, singling us out as disruptive, religious frauds.

I look up at the roof: ornate carvings of biblical figures all staring down at us, and asking why we're here, in their house, disrespecting their ancestors.

A few moments later, a fat, bald guy approaches us and says, 'can you stop being so disruptive please, or I'll have to ask you to leave.'

'But God reminds me eh ma granddad,' Specks replies.

'Can A come and meet the big man before we head,' Jimmy says. 'Because A've always wanted tae meet the cunt eh.'

The man smiles, then looks up to the heavens, before fixing his attention on Jimmy.

'Please refrain from using blasphemy in this house of God…you don't have to go anywhere to meet him, young man. He's all around you.'

'Eh must be a fat bastard then,' replies Jimmy, again producing laughter from all of us.

Our man seems unsure what to say next.

'Who's this fuckin secular by the way?' Jimmy says.

'Please, can I remind you not to – '

'It better no huv been that cunt secular who pit those leaflits through ma door.'

'Sorry, I'm going to have to ask you to leave.'

'Tell secular tae stoap comin tae ma fuckin door then. Nane eh ma family are bothered.'

Then there was more confrontation, involving more disparaging comments about this guy secular – who Jimmy was now absolutely convinced was to blame – and even a slightly hairy moment that could quite easily have turned into something physical between Jimmy and another member of the congregation, before we eventually voluntarily leave and swiftly cross the road to buy some crisps.

I'll never forget crossing the road that day and glancing at Specks. He was all the time looking at Jimmy, hoping he would say something nice: something about his performance in the church. All he really wanted was confirmation that he'd done ok. Not even brilliantly, but just ok. So when he said to Jimmy, 'that wis funny as fuck likes,' I waited for the response in trepidation, suddenly feeling for Specks. And then a deep rooted sorrow for his current predicament and a real hatred for Jimmy that he had this emotional power over a friend of mine.

When no answer came I repeated what Specks had said, trying to evoke some kind of response.

'That wis funny as fuck likes.'

Jimmy then looked at me and after smiling, said, 'aye, you wur fuckin hilarious mate.'

I then said, 'you wur mental Specks,' but this went unanswered.

Some memories from your youth stick with you: strangely it's usually the most trivial of things. However, this memory wasn't like that; this was a serious thing to retain all these years, a really poignant moment in our youth. This was the day I realised that Jimmy Stokes had a grip of Specks' entire future, and when I received a phone call two decades later to say he was dead, I knew it was suicide, and I knew it was partly because of that day.

*

Jane has an appointment to get her eyes tested today. Before nodding off last night, she jokingly asked how I'd like the secretarial look. But as she said this I was looking at an open punnet of red grapes leaning over the edge of the bedside cabinet and thinking about the time Specks got cataract surgery on his eyes.

He had been on the NHS waiting list for over a year, but had finally managed to get an appointment. My mum had said it obviously wasn't deemed priority so he shouldn't have got too downhearted about the long wait.

Naturally, we wanted to be supportive, because the word *friend* constitutes more than just immoral acts of behaviour towards anyone unlucky enough to be in our way. It also meant a bus journey for Noggin and me.

Obviously we're all praying Jimmy has better things to do than support his friend having an operation. But he does know about it…that reality we can't hide from.

The appointment is at 11am on London Road, so we decided to leave at 9am. This meant we could get off on Princess Street, do a bit of window shopping, and even have adequate time to pick up Specks' favourite football magazine on the way down Leith Walk – hoping to arrive just after eleven.

Hopping off the bus at the West End, Noggin says to me he wants to look at something in Waterstones. Apparently Mrs Hindley – or *Jugs* as we called her – had told him of a book about some high school *prodigy* by a foreign author called *Hermann Hesse*. Of course when he said this I instinctively looked over my shoulder, just to check nobody had overheard him, but actually, in retrospect, I remember feeling this overwhelming warmth towards him for feeling able to say such a thing to me.

Noggin had been taking extra English lessons and was perpetually paranoid about leaving school, because sometimes Jimmy lingered about to watch a fight – or even start one. Anyone knows that unless you're in detention – which of course you brag about – leaving school an hour late means you've been staying behind. This kind of behaviour deserves a slap in Jimmy's eyes. Studying hard during the day and partaking in Jimmy's way of life at night: what an oxymoron Noggin's life was.

Noggin looked at me and said, 'Six fuckin ninety nine? Where's the great thief when yae need him maist?'

'Gettin eez eyes fixed so he has a better success rate…'

Noggin laughs, before glancing at me then furtively at the counter assistant. I know he won't do it because it's not his style, but I look out for the security guard anyway – just in case he's thinking of temporarily standing in for Specks.

Obviously he bottled it in the end, because we've all got our place in life, and stealing isn't his…he definitely thought about it though: I could see it in his eyes.

After leaving Waterstones empty handed, we listened to some music in HMV, had a look at Timberland boots in USC, and then walked through Princess Street Gardens – because there were always tramps sleeping and we found winding them up entertaining.

Finally grabbing a milkshake each from McDonald's, we made our way down Leith Walk, and turned onto London Road – not forgetting to first purchase *GOAL* from the newsagents just across from St James Centre.

Specks said 'thank you,' instead of 'cheers,' when we gave him the magazine. It's perfectly logical that he might have had a near death experience mid-operation, and came out the other side a changed person, after some floating God had absolved him of all his sins. It was probably just the anaesthetic, though.

He went on to tell us that the specialist said he'd be out within a few hours and he wouldn't have to wear such thick lenses anymore. He thought this might give him a better chance with Donna – who we all called dirty Donna. We didn't have the heart to tell him we had overheard her calling him a stocker and a weirdo in Maths just the other day.

Jimmy

We sit on the edge of his bed discussing yesterday's swimming class: Sara Patterson's swimming costume had ripped up the middle and we had seen absolutely everything, because it was when she was standing on the diving board, hands in the air. A sublime moment.

On further investigation from our P.E teacher it looked like someone had cut it slightly when she was in the toilet, leaving the lining very vulnerable. It seems a bit of a coincidence that Sara Patterson just happened to have the biggest tits in the class.

Specks is sitting up in his bed trying to imitate Sara Patterson's feeble attempt to cover herself up, when suddenly we hear a familiar voice at reception – changing the atmosphere from warm to bitter cold.

'A tolt thum no tae lit um in,' Specks mumbles, forlornly.

'Ye said that! What if they tell um?' I open the curtain slightly so we can hear better, and it seems the receptionist is holding her ground. Then we hear Jimmy say, 'A'm no a fuckin visitor: A just wantae ask um how many fingers A'm hawdin up.'

I turn to look at Noggin and Specks; Noggin is laughing and Specks is smiling – a mixture of recognising the hilarity of the situation and an acknowledged reticence at being the butt of the joke.

Eventually we hear a man's voice asking what is going on, and then what sounds like Jimmy squaring up to his assailant, before the guy retorts that he'll phone the police.

There's an anxious few seconds and then we hear Jimmy shouting, 'A just wanted tae gee a present tae ma fuckin blind mate,' before slamming the door behind him.

Jimmy this, Jimmy that

We look at each other, and then smile. We look at each other again and then simultaneously burst out laughing.

What's puzzled me ever since was what Jimmy had brought: were his intentions genuinely altruistic, and he'd really brought a gift for Specks? Even if it was something insulting like a large pair of glasses, had we really prevented Jimmy from showing some affection? After all, irrespective of the outcome, he had made the effort to come. He even remembered the time and place. Was Jimmy a real friend after all, or was it just a case of an opportunist taking the opportunity to have some fun? It's possible he didn't have anything at all and this was just a ploy to get past the receptionist.

On the other hand, he might just have had a punnet of grapes.

I open Luke's door and feel a pang of fear. Every morning I wake before him I'm faced with the same devastating prospect: what if he doesn't wake up? What if the Gods have taken him from us?

Only when he stirs, can I finally breathe.
Only when he stirs, can I finally move on.
Only when he stirs, can I finally be thankful for another day.

The ultimate fear is your children being taken before you.
You've experienced the stages of life, and so must they.

Only when he stirs, can you appreciate what you have.

And soon there will be two.

*

Life is split into three stages; being a child, when naivety makes the world think you're cute; being a teenager, when every noun starts and ends with a fuck; and being an adult, when you're blessed with thinking for yourself.

I live in the third stage now, but I can still smell the second stage; every confrontation I witnessed, every waft of illegal smoke. Jimmy will always be there, in the back of my head. The boys also, in all our glory, but predominantly Jimmy; that one goes down in folklore as another scratch on the post, the post of people destined to never taste the third stage of life.

6

On this misty, bitter cold evening, as we slowly wander up the bumpy incline, the normally loquacious Noggin is silent and composed. He walks with the precision of a tight-rope performer; meticulous, fastidious and perpetually focused. I watch him take in his surroundings, his ordinary every day thoughts amalgamated into one singular focal point: Jimmy's plan. His hands are rough, as though he's spent hours fortifying them with sandpaper, preparing them for use. His skin is pale, and although one could easily put this down to sleep deprivation, somehow I doubt this. There's normally joviality between us, thankfulness for like-minded people, but this usual energy has evaporated into nothingness: disappeared into the night.

Nothingness is possibly the only word suitable enough to describe his countenance – and mine for that matter – and looking away from him I attempt to focus on this particular emotion; analysing, evaluating and attempting to understand it. I then try and compare the feeling in my stomach with an incident a few weeks earlier, when after a football-related dispute – witnessed by more people than felt comfortable – Dave Smith had asked me for a square-go after class. I remember a sudden weight in the pit of my stomach, having witnessed him annihilating a sixth year only the day before; and of course, you never say no to a fight; not unless you want to be labelled a *Sap* or a *Chicken*. After-school fights are never life threatening, but Dave's a big guy for his age and he also has what is often referred to as a 'metal chin'. Obviously feeling confident, he had taunted me for the rest of the period with eyes, fingers, and even the odd note. A sense of foreboding had followed me around until the bell rang, but any altercation never actually materialised, because I'd quite brilliantly used my initiative, throwing a *soggy* at Mr Kerr, and then forcing Danny Loven to grass me up – leading to detention after school. This was the perfect plan, because why would Dave hang around so long for a fight that nobody would witness?

The next again day he came up to me and said, 'nae hard feelings, mate.' I didn't actually respond, only smiled, because Noggin had told me on the way to school that Dave had been warned by someone he was getting a bit too big for his own boots.

Jimmy Stokes might well have inadvertently saved my skin that day, but as we're approaching the high-rise flats I recognise that this near miss was a mixture of personal pragmatism and association with the school's top boy. Trying to compare the aforementioned with what lies ahead is futile, because I'm not walking out of a classroom kicking and punching until a teacher separates us; I'm about to embark on a mission that pragmatism doesn't factor in, nor the fact of being a friend of Jimmy's. In school there's always someone nearby ready to throw in the towel for you, but in Peebo's flat, the only towel available will be the one used to clean up blood.

From about fifty metres away I enjoy the entirety of Jimmy's appearance from a completely different perspective. I've never felt the need for his experience the way I feel it now. There'll be no show of indifference or a brilliantly constructed façade, because this time I will listen to what he says; I will pray he can deliver.

Jimmy had shaved his head. Whilst we were shivering in our bedrooms, he was standing in front of his mirror, replicating a scene from *American History X*. I would have thought that copying them was respecting them, but what did I know. He was also wearing a leather jacket because his cousin Alec always said leather is better protection from a knife. This doesn't exactly fill me with confidence, because of all the times he's said this, this is the first time he's actually worn one.

Arriving at the big industrial metal door, a black cat is staring at me. Not at the other three, just at me. I've never been one for premonitions, but this cat seems to be telling me something.

The council haven't fixed the door for over a million years, so overcoming our first obstacle of entry isn't a problem and Jimmy puts his finger to his lips, ushering us inside.

Enduring a mixture of dog shit, stale beer and what smells like a dead body hidden somewhere in the vicinity, we collectively stop, having recognised that no dialogue has passed between us yet. It's approximately seven minutes since I left my house, and I haven't once opened my mouth – except to breathe in the cold air.

The following piece of silent theatre then takes place: Noggin looks at Jimmy's eyes, which appear to

Jimmy

be bloodshot and evidently palpating – a clear indication that he's been using narcotics prior to our meeting – then shakes his head in distress; I look at Jimmy to confirm Noggin's suspicions, and then nod my head in agreement, but at the same time divert my gaze towards Specks, who's holding a black marker and scribbling on the wall.

Four guys, tools at the ready, and Specks thought it most appropriate to draw a giant cock on the wall. Must have been premeditated, because who brings a permanent marker to a war zone unless they intend on leaving behind a mark?

*

Wasn't until I saw Kevin wearing a suit and tie that I truly acknowledged the significance of the occasion.

The service was held at Warriston Crematorium, and unlike my Uncle Davie's funeral – which hundreds had attended only a matter of months ago – it was perfectly evident from the moment we walked through the door that this funeral service was for someone very few admired.

The chapel was bereft of people, and apart from the three of us, there was only another five in attendance; a slender woman – his girlfriend, I assume – clutching onto two grubby looking kids, and two men who looked like they were rejoicing rather than mourning.

The bag of bones was aggressively holding back her tears, and on perusing the constitution of the two kids, there didn't seem to be much weight on them either. Wearing brown trousers, a hoody, and sporting a pair of Nike Air Max trainers, she was more suited to a meeting with a dealer than her boyfriend's meeting with the grim reaper. Her rotting teeth and pale complexion told you everything you needed to know about Specks' lifestyle over the years. The overuse of narcotics meant she had a very nervous countenance; fidgeting and watching the rest of the small burial party with suspicion. Kevin very cleverly pointed out that Specks most likely had many enemies – the type of people who would have no moral scruples about upsetting an occasion such as this, and glancing again at the other two attendants, I began to wonder if she was in danger… if *we* were in danger.

After the body had been cremated, the two men shook hands, and it became suddenly evident that they were there as witnesses. They must have been sent to confirm the news, and this type of horribly immoral behaviour is something I hope I never have to witness again.

On leaving, they approached the bag of bones, and the taller, angrier looking one said, 'git oan wi yer life love…'

There was no response, but it was obvious who they were, and what they were capable of.

In the end, I felt I owed it to Specks to rub the younger kids head on the way out and mutter, 'your dad was a good man.'

As we walked up the gravel pathway, Kevin said, 'Was he?'

I didn't answer this tongue-in-cheek remark, because I felt that even the most unfortunate of people deserve a certain measure of respect, at least until we were off the grounds anyway.

We enjoyed our own mini wake in a nearby pub.

After a painstakingly boring conversation about the ramifications of bringing another life into the world, we finished our drinks and left. Turning the corner we almost ran into the bereaving mother and her two children. She was wheezing like someone with emphysema, having just tossed a finished cigarette onto the ground, and then she stopped dead and looked at us.

'Ye kent ma Gavin?'

'Ye...we did,' answered Kevin.

She took a step closer to me, her rotting teeth in full view.

'Ye wur right. What ye said back there...he wis a good man...and they've taken um fi me.'

She then looked at me and smiled, before shouting something threatening in the direction of her children – who had started to make their own way along the road without her.

'Told you,' I said to Kevin, who smiled and then started laughing.

'They've taken um fi me,' I mutter to myself, thinking that I would have liked to sit down with her, ask what his life was like. Why he did what he did.

We watched the remnants of Specks' legacy fading into the open space, losing their grip on the burning body, the proximity of the pastoral tributes, and having to accept the closing of his existence. Fortunately for him though, his legacy would live on through those children, now lagging behind their mother and trying to keep up with a woman desperate for her next fix.

'I told her.'
'Who?'
'Jennifer.'
'Your boss, Jennifer?'
'How many other Jennifer's do you know?'
'You told her what?'
'That I'm pregnant again!'
'Ok…and how did she take it?'
'Well, I didn't actually tell her.'
'You just said you did.'

'I went to work yesterday and she glared at me, and then looked at my breasts, before turning me sideways. She's got three children herself. '

'So…again…how did she take it?'

Jane took a moment from clipping Luke's toenails and looked at me; pensive, as though she was actually looking through me, searching for a picture of the exact conversation.

'After indignantly admitting her disappointment at my stupidity – considering we had just finished preliminary discussions about me being the manager of her new shop – she apologized, congratulated me, and then offered her support.'

'Kind of her to call you stupid.'

'She's a business woman. I should take her response as a compliment. Besides, she said I'll always be welcome back.'

'That's nice.'

'I know what you're thinking…'

But I've lost interest in the conversation, because sitting on the couch beside her is the order of service, which she's perversely using as a deposit station for Luke's nail clippings. The square picture in the middle of the paper is slowly metamorphosing into a younger Gavin Scott, and the writing underneath the picture is changing from two names to one. I no longer see a Gavin Scott; I see a boy called Specks; a picture of youthfulness and mischief, disruption and contempt. This person is looking back at me with eagerness, quietly awaiting my next move.

7

A seagull, hungry and restless, perched on top of a lamppost and illuminated by the flickering light, glares at an industrial bin; a man, suffering from insomnia, fills up his petrol tank at the twenty four hour garage; an errant drunken lady stumbles in the opposite direction from home; a couple, move quickly in the missionary position, both guilty of infidelity; the ground floor of a high-rise tenement building, Peebo's four assailants are poised, ready to make their move. As a species we all move simultaneously, etching different words into the history books.

I'm in a coma but I'm still awake. The sentence, 'the lift is too dodgy, lits take the stairs,' only just resonates with my brain.

I look at my weapon. Take comfort in the fact Jimmy entrusted me with an inexperienced piece of weaponry: a virgin in battle. In potentially less than five minutes, I'm going to have to muster together some form of sense memory from when I played *rounders* as a youngster, and force it through the air – imagining Peebo's head as the ball. This very barbaric reality sends a shiver down my spine, and I clench my fists together, almost dropping the bat to the ground.

Jimmy

There's a dead man walking...there's a dead man walking...

We're heading for floor five, flat thirteen. Every floor is partitioned by plastic revolving doors that look about as sturdy as a fart in the wind. Just as we're passing a sign that says Three, a man with a Rottweiler materialises from the other side of the partition. Imagine you're a neighbour in a building that holds around three hundred residents, and in the middle of the night four teenagers are climbing the stairs, carrying weapons, quite obviously not just on their way to a chess tournament. What do you do? Do you phone the police? Would you challenge said criminals – taking into consideration it's four against one and you might very well end up lying on the stairs with your dog licking blood from your face? On the other hand, how do you feel about this type of thing occurring in your place of repose? Or is there some kind of tacit agreement that what happens outside of your floor stays outside your floor? Or is there an even simpler solution: this type of heinous behaviour is a regular occurrence in this building and considering your neighbour on one side is a drug dealer, and the lady opposite runs an illegal brothel – not to mention the boy directly next to you who talks so much about the British National Party that you're starting to wonder if he's harbouring German fugitives. Taking all this into account, we probably don't seem that suspicious. Or of course there could be an even more obvious answer: there's currently a warrant out for your arrest and you're presently crashing on a friend's sofa, so are just delighted it's not the police. There's perspective in everything.

Jimmy this, Jimmy that

The guy has his hood up, and stops to pick up his dog. He glares at us through beady eyes – meaning we stop as a unit in preparation for any potential threat. A smile begins to form, and then he laughs, places his dog gently on the ground, and pulls a joint out from behind his ear – handing it to Jimmy. Does he recognise him? Or recognise the situation? Does he know where we're going? Has the whole building heard of our impending attack? Or is this just a peace offering?

Jimmy pulls a lighter from his pocket, and sparks the joint. The boy laughs again and mutters, 'git that wee joint in ye, boys. Nout like a bit eh fuckin weed before a rumble.' The inhabitant of floor number three shows us his teeth, and I'm beginning to wonder if the government have put a dentistry injunction on the entire building, when he stumbles into the wall, before sacrilegiously kicking his dog down the stairs.

As we move through the revolving doors into floor number five, Jimmy aggressively tightens the grip on his blade. An eerie colour permeates the walls of this floor, almost as though Peebo intentionally requested it from the council because it's the scariest: a dark, thick looking red colour; the colour of human blood.

Jimmy is bobbing his head back and forward and muttering something under his breath. He then starts off by saying, 'when we git in there boys, jist remember, dinnae act scared. It shows a sign eh weakness.'

Jesus Christ, it's not a football match, Jimmy. This isn't a pep talk. We're all fucking terrified.

'Yer gonnae be oan yer aine.'

I thought we were in this together?

'This isnae boys fi the fuckin school. This is the real deal.'

I'm pretty certain we've established that much.

'A'm no really sure what these pricks'll be hinkin. They might even be expectin us, but once we fuckin smash thum, A want ye tae steal whatever ye kin.'

Fight and then steal? If I get the opportunity to steal, it won't be possessions: it'll be distance in metres away from this building.

'Forgit aboot material possessions.'

Did Jimmy just sound remotely intelligent for a second there?

'A want fuckin weed and pills. Now here's what's gonnae happen…A'm gonnae tap the cunts door.'

A far more cordial approach than I would have expected.

'And when the cunt answers, we're gonnae steam in.'

No game plan, just steam in?

'Remember, they might be ready. And if they are, we've goat a wee bit eh a problem.'

You think?

'Now…are we fuckin ready tae do these cunts?'

'Cunts' in plural, assuming the very amiable friend is still there.

'Boys, lits make history.'

*

Jimmy this, Jimmy that

On this somewhat cold morning, I pass a turquoise coloured Honda with the passenger seat window shattered, and on glancing inside I notice a gaping hole where the car radio would have been the night before. I'm on my way to meet the guys at the corner, and on clutching the strap of my school bag I start thinking about how yesterday's trials went for the fourth year football team: I think I played pretty well. Everyone there was so desperate to play up front – because they're all narcissistic and hungry for glory – but I've always wanted to be a defensive Midfielder. Protecting my own goal has inherently felt like a priority every time I walk onto the pitch, so taking the aforementioned egotistical approach of my competitors into account, I'm almost guaranteed a place in the first team.

After enumerating the definitive candidates in my head and calculating I'm probably the sixth or seventh best player in the year, I start pondering whether Brendan Smith's brutal tackle on Gary Tanner was deliberate or not, when in the distance I notice a girl walking towards me.

It might be winter, but judging by her decision to actually wear clothes, I can tell she's different from other girls. From afar she looks a bit smaller than me, with dirty blond hair and what we often describe in school as 'a decent set'. She's currently tying her hair back – flicking it from side to side like they do in the Head and Shoulders advert – and evidently slowing down. On the other hand, it's highly plausible her waning speed is just part of my fantasy, because the slow-motion girl is the most attractive.

Fortunately, for the sake of my sanity, it turns out I'm more than accurate, because, in fact, she's actually stopped and is extracting something from her bag.

Jimmy

She distrustfully snaps her head back to eye level and catches me looking. Did she just look at me? Or was it just her surroundings? I wouldn't exactly describe this area as one for sight-seeing. Maybe she's noticed I've also slowed down and is a bit suspicious? Maybe she wants me to talk to her? Initiate some sort of flirtatious conversation. Maybe she's also fantasising about me from afar? I can't flick my hair like she did, but I can wiggle my shoulders, which will undoubtedly show I'm not intimidated by her approaching beauty whatsoever.

So I stop dead, pulling my shoulders back in preparation to execute the walk then shoulder wiggle, walk then shoulder wiggle, but don't actually move at all, because the following dawns on me; we all know about Jimmy's sexual exploits, his confidence with the other sex, and his ability to brag about 'experience', but what about me? Well, apart from the hand-job Lizzy Bartram gave me in the boy's toilets – which went terribly wrong because she told me I should have been able to last longer than I did – I'm a fully confessed virgin. That's right, the big V. I know I'm only fourteen, but when you hung about with someone who had been with half the girls in our area, it made you feel inadequate. Not that I should be ashamed of this really…Jimmy probably had countless sexually transmitted diseases. I'm on the very periphery of being labelled a Mormon: someone who chooses to wait until they're married. Of course I do have the advantage of deceit – which most of the fourth and fifth years use. Nobody in my year is a virgin anymore. They all slept with someone during the summer holidays, staying up north with their gran, or on some unforgettable night out with their older cousin. Obviously, if I have to

Jimmy this, Jimmy that

resort to lying I will, but I'm also not going to just sleep with one of the slags in the school purely to heighten my reputation. Like Noggin, I've got standards…and this girl, by the looks of it, ticks every box.

Predictably, however, it seems my chances are fading, because she's started walking again, and has actually just crossed the road. Let's hope it's not because of me?

The thing she took out of her bag was a hat, which she's now wearing. It covers most of her head and part of her face, so I can only really make out one side of her.

Choosing not to accept defeat, I decide to cross the road also. Obviously this could look a bit desperate – or a bit perverted – but connections like this don't come along very often. This girl could be the one to take away my V and change it to an S for *Shagger*. From this view she doesn't look like anyone in my year either, which is a massive bonus. Maybe she's in the year above, like Claire Donaldson, who seems to always be on my mind when my bedroom lights go out.

Here's the problem: what do I say to her?

'Dae ye come here often?'

She would answer, 'where, the middle eh the fuckin road?'

She probably wouldn't swear though…she doesn't look the type.

What about, 'that's a nice hat?'

But she might just answer, 'sorry, dae A ken you?'

Or she might be from one of the richer schools and say, 'sorry, do I know you?'

I could just do nothing, smile at her, and ensure I'm here at this exact time tomorrow, because let's be honest, that's probably what will happen. I'll no doubt just let her walk right past me...as always.

But wait a minute; she's taking her hat off. Surely that's a sign? She might just have an itchy head, but on the other hand she might want me to scratch it for her. Flick my hand through her hair, rubbing my thumb against her scalp, and then lifting up her top, so she can show me her...no, it's a bit cold for that. Or maybe there's a spider inside and I could be her hero; pretend it's a rare poisonous one and save her from certain death. Or I could even, but holy shit, it's Tiny: Noggin's sister. How did I not notice that? And now that I see her a little closer, she looks angry. Is she angry at me? What if by some telepathic brilliance she knew I was fantasising about her? What if she managed to get inside my head and could see my failed hand-job with Lizzy Bartram, or the fact that I spoke about her as the one. I really need to get a grip of myself: try and act like nothing has upset my equilibrium...

'Hiya Tiny...eh...how's yer...eh...'

She stops and says, 'how's ma what?'

Shit, what was I going to ask?

'Eh...yer brother?'

'Kevin?'

'What?'

'What ye oan aboot?'

'Eh...A was just askin aboot Noggin. How's he...eh...takin it?'

'Takin what? And his names Kevin...'

She then saunters off, but not without grimacing at me first.

What just happened there? What was I going to say to her…how's your vagina? Was I really about to ask that? Am I really that paranoid in front of females that the only thing I could regurgitate was the most insulting question of all? Thank goodness she cut me off. And how is he taking it? That's even worse.

That's not the biggest issue here though. Surely the biggest thing to take into consideration is the fact that I was fantasising about my best friends little sister. Not big sister: little sister; baby sister. What if she tells him I was gawking at her?

*

Noggin and I are doing some reconnaissance work for Jimmy.

He's going to *tan a hoose.*

We've been watching this older lady for a few days now. She stays on the bottom floor and enjoys a pretty predictable schedule: leaves around 9am and returns somewhere between 2pm and 3pm – carrying shopping bags from Marks and Spencer's. I use the word older instead of old, because she might only actually be about 50. She's definitely a spinster though. Either that or the husband is away somewhere. She doesn't act like the married type. Sometimes you can tell if somebody's independent. The way they walk, and a certain countenance that suggests they obstinately refer to nobody but themselves.

Jimmy

Jimmy has chosen this particular house because there's a serious shrubbery problem. It's only surprising the council haven't landed the whole stair with a fine under the 'Safe protection of our properties act 1995,' or however they choose to categorize this lack of regular attendance to the surrounding greenery. Usually it's a breakdown in communication with the other members of the building, or just no system in place for what has now become an obviously arduous task.

It's late Saturday morning and we're trying our best not to look conspicuous. For two fourteen year olds in an area where most fourteen year olds do nothing but get up to mischief, this isn't as easy as it looks, so we keep our eye line mainly on each other.

The initial plan is to kick the ball back and forward until an overzealous volley forces it to land in the front garden. Marching through the gate with confidence, I will then scope out the front side of the house – whilst ostensibly collecting my football. For safety, we might do this twice, just in case she doesn't stick to her routine at the weekend, and we just happen to be in a blind spot the first time we check. To avoid contrived behaviour we ensure it's at least five minutes between each wayward kick.

Once this part of the operation is complete, I will kick the ball into the air and scream the code word 'EMPTY'. This works really well, because not only does it confirm that, from the front viewpoint, the house is bereft of proprietors, it is also a well-used word in football for clearing the ball out of your own box, so the raising of the voice will undoubtedly be associated with football. Believe it or not, it's probably a good thing if someone does look out their window, because that will help to confirm our innocence.

After two successful runs, I pick up the football, kick it high into the air, and then scream, 'EMPTY.'

Then there's the second part: 'kin A speak tae Billy, please.' This involves tapping on the person's door – or ringing the buzzer if the stair door is closed, which is obviously the least potentially intimidating choice. However, the rules are clear; if the stair door is open, approach the house door directly, because, without personal engagement, anyone at home might think it's just the postman and ignore it. If they do answer, you say, 'kin A speak tae Billy, please. He said eh wis gonnae lend eez his fitbaw boots.'

If nobody answers, I go back onto the street and shout, 'EMPTY,' again.

This signal gives Specks permission to start his reconnaissance work on the back windows. His approach is less personal than ours and involves a slingshot loaded with a small stone. Pulling the sling back and releasing it with velocity, the stone flies through the air and hits the kitchen window. A smallish stone is enough to crack the glass but not smash it. It's also enough to create severe interior noise but not exterior. This way the neighbours will only suspect it's the noise of a starting car, or a failing engine. Then Specks will move from behind the bush and stand in the middle of the garden, pretending to look for something, but all the time keeping his eye on the window of the house. If nobody looks out, the operation is a go. If they do, however, Specks will be forced to improvise. The outcome of this isn't a big issue, because by then it's obvious the operation is not going to go ahead anyway, so no premeditated plans are put in place. On one occasion, an older man – who was supposed to be out – opened his window to see who had cracked it with a stone, and Specks pointed to his right and brilliantly said, 'they went that wey. A'm jist searchin fur a bit eh ma anus.' With contempt and confusion, the old man closed his window without response. What could he reply to that anyway?

If nobody does appear, our only job from then on is to *keep shoaty*, for police, neighbours, and the old lady arriving home earlier than expected.

Obviously there wasn't a democratic approach to the delegating of tasks, but if there had been, it would have been a unanimous decision that both Jimmy and Specks were better equipped to be the ones in the back garden, preparing for entry. One would probably then predict Specks being the one who would enter the premises – based on his experience – but this wouldn't actually be the case, because Jimmy will be desperate to decide what stays and what goes in his bag. Jimmy is the one who sells the stuff.

Because Noggin is the brains of the bunch, and I'm glued to his hip, it was our job yesterday to visit the back garden and attempt to ascertain any problem with regards entry. We had initially concluded that the windows were too high off the ground and this might in fact put a stop to the whole operation, but then I noticed an abandoned wheel, partly hidden under the long grass. This could be propped against the wall, allowing easy access for Jimmy through the kitchen window. Obviously we were relying on this wheel still being there the day after, but it didn't look to us like it was ready to be transported any time soon, because on closer inspection there where snails using it as a hideaway. It had obviously been deemed obsolete long ago.

For a teenager, nothing is obsolete.

It might have looked like a haphazard attempt to get the attention of someone inside, but the accuracy of Specks' slingshot was actually of vast importance, because the vulnerability of the window would aid Jimmy's entry. This being the 90's, the majority of households didn't have double glazing or locks on their windows, so a simple repetitive tapping of a hammer on the already cracked area would mean the glass eventually giving way and creating a big enough hole for a hand to slip through and deftly open it from the inside.

When it came to house robbery, Jimmy was as pedantic as a hygiene officer and surprisingly respectful of property. He replaced plants, closed cupboards, and even shouted at Specks for dragging dirt through the carpet.

I often wondered if Jimmy had been victim of a really brutal break-in one day – the pilferers leaving a mess everywhere – and his perpetual need to replicate but deviate from this was a mixture of what goes around comes around, his obvious instincts for barbarity, and an attempt to eradicate the effects from his memory by doing the job properly.

And so there was a process.

Once Jimmy was successfully inside, Specks would go through the process of counting from 1 to 100, and then furtively disappear.

After receiving the code word, 'OUT', from Specks – another football related term – Noggin and I would then nonchalantly sit on the fence of the front garden and look for possible antagonists. Any sign of police, we would smash one of the front windows and run like fuck. This would let Jimmy know he was in a potentially sticky situation and at the same time hopefully leave the police with competing priorities; chase the window smashers, or follow the tipoff from the neighbours. You might think this plan sounds a little simplistic, but the one time this happened, the police (both of them!) chased me and Noggin.

After about ten minutes, when we were pretty confident Jimmy had collected the valuables, made sure their personal space wasn't too violated and successfully climbed back out the window, over the fence and away, Noggin kicked the ball down the street and I ran after it – wondering what Jimmy had managed to get this time.

Fortunately, Jimmy only required us for this type of operation about half a dozen times, but every time I was left with a feeling of having been violated myself; not only did we never find out exactly what he had taken – or who he had sold it to – we were never given a cut of the money.

8

Deftly, like a hunting spider approaching its prey, my right hand creeps slowly up my neck, passing the jaw-line without intrusion, before resting on a bump just below the temple. My index finger taps the area in question, again and again, recognising the anomaly in my normally smooth complexion.

I open my eyes. I seem to be sitting awkwardly. A shooting pain coming from the side of my face makes me clench my teeth. The fact that I'm still functioning properly fills me with gladness, but this pleasure soon evaporates, because the bump on my head confirms I must have been hit and therefore involved in some sort of physical confrontation. Is this heaven or hell? Am I still part of the human race? Or am I sitting in Purgatory, reading *Dante's Inferno,* wishing I'd behaved better during my short stay on planet earth? Wherever I am, it's certainly no utopia.

Smoke permeates the vicinity like slow moving clouds or the somnolent harr over a short stretch of water. This abstract description of a chilly autumn afternoon might sound like one of Scotland's rural landscapes, but it's actually just smoke from cigarettes and joints, because this is Peebo's flat, and the ambience in here will never make the cover of a holiday brochure.

Jimmy

I attempt to brush some of the mist away and notice three people sitting on the couch opposite me. This must be Jimmy and the skinheads, but why are they not fighting to the death? Why isn't there shouting and swearing? Punching and kicking? There's already so much about this situation I don't like. I look to my left and Specks is tied to a chair. What the fuck is going on? And where's Noggin? Why is Specks tied to that chair, and where are his glasses? What have they done to his hair? Is this some kind of dream? Why would Noggin just leave me here? Where's all the blood? What happened to the animosity? The only picture of brutality I can see is Specks strapped to a chair, head resting against his chest as though suffering from post-interrogation syndrome. Everything else seems jovial, as if this was a party and not a battle scene. Have I been out cold, and if so, for how long? Is Noggin dead? Or did he escape? I need to try and piece together the little information I can remember; we came up the steps, past the crazy guy and his dog, and then stopped not far away from Peebo's door; Jimmy gave his speech and we collectively moved forward – like a cavalry…but then what happened? The bump on the side of my head is definitive evidence that somewhere along the line I must have been hit, but the fact I can't remember anything else means I could either be suffering from concussion, or I was hit as soon as I entered and have been in a coma ever since. I feel ok; sore but present, drowsy but alert, inquisitive but terrified. The blow was low enough to cause a tumour-like lump on the top of my cheek, but fortunately not high enough to give me brain damage: at least not immediately. What the fuck is going on then?

Glancing out the window it still seems to be dark. This means it's obviously still the middle of the night, but because it doesn't get light until around 7am, I could have easily been lying here for hours. The stillness should fill me with comfort, but instead fills me with a sense of trepidation.

I decide to take a moment to gather my surroundings – just in case I need to have my faculties about me sooner than required – when a whimpering sound suddenly belches from Specks. At least he's still alive…

A shaky hand then slowly materialises through the smoke, holding a joint. I look to the ground and notice my baseball bat resting against the wall, unused. This confirms to me that whatever battle I was involved in, I obviously lost.

'Wakey, wakey,' a voice says.

I reluctantly take the joint from what appears to be the hand of Peebo's friend, before glancing over at Specks again. He's slightly lifted up his head and I can just make out a tear rolling down his cheek. What does this mean? And what's happened to him? What's with the duct tape and those pliers on the table? I open my mouth to ask what they've done with Specks but nothing comes out.

I don't put the joint in my mouth and nobody seems to disagree with this. I merely hold it, allowing for the miniature piece of lava at the top to slowly burn down the paper. I'm trying to ascertain if I'm still involved in something? Is this similar to that moment in the war, on Christmas day, when everyone dropped their weapons and played football, showing a very distant hint of altruism and empathy in amongst the massacre? I often wonder if the team who won the game also won the war, and maybe the outcome gave them a moral advantage. Maybe the team who could hold their nerve on the football pitch went back to the fighting with a renewed hope? Maybe there was more at stake than just the opportunity to win something that didn't involve killing. Maybe this game of football on Christmas day has more historical significance than the history books report. But does this mean I will go back to fighting, just like they did? Is this just an interlude? Should I lunge for my baseball bat in preparation? Or is this it? Like the signing of the armistice, has this war ended until further disputes arise? Is there nothing else happening here apart from three guys having a smoke and some poor bastard tied to a chair? Should I just get up and leave? Would anyone even care? Do I have any moral obligation towards Specks? Even if I do, what can I realistically do about it?

Quickly deciding this is one story I'd rather be prematurely written out of, I send a signal to my brain, but this signal is declined and my legs don't respond. They seem to know better. They think someone will oppose my decision to get up and go, and if there's no correlation between the emotional and physical trigger in your faculties, something is clearly wrong; either I'm dead or my moral responsibilities are outweighing everything else.

Apparently I'm going nowhere.

I look at Jimmy and he's smiling. There's an evident cut on his lip. It's difficult to know if this is just an illusion – part of me hoping he was damaged in some way for dragging us into this mess in the first place. The other

Jimmy this, Jimmy that

two are smiling also, and from the angle of their heads, I know it's not at the television, something one of them have said, or even the most enjoyable side effect of marijuana, the giggles. They are, in fact, smiling at Specks, because he's just attempted some sort of impulsive escape, and on violently shaking the chair from side to side has toppled over and banged the side of his head on the floor. The duct tape over his mouth explains his lack of communication, and my impulsive reaction is to move and help him up, but again, my legs refuse.

How can this be funny? What is there to fucking laugh about? I want to scream at these three people. I want to pick up my bat and ram it down Jimmy's throat. How can he betray Specks like this? How can he sit there and watch him suffer? The boy worships Jimmy. He looks up to him and follows his every move. Does everything he's ordered to without inner indignation. Noggin and I secretly despise Jimmy, but Specks genuinely admires him.

I send a signal to my legs again, and this time they respond. The skinheads might have fought their battle, but mine has just begun.

I'm just about to grab for the baseball bat when the three heads turn in my direction. I realise what I'm about to do and the possible ramifications. I recognise that certain provocations are better left to people more equipped, but I'm all there is.

For once in my life I feel pious.

I look at Specks lying on the floor, helpless and inert, and prepare for attack. However, my compassionate intentions are brought to a halt and I find my body stopping in mid-air – the perfect parody of a statue – because the

Jimmy

three skinheads are looking past me, at something else, and Peebo has just muttered, 'ye took yer fuckin time wee man.'

I slump back down on the couch, having only actually moved a matter of inches, because Noggin has just walked into the room holding three cups of tea or is it coffee?

I sit and think for a few seconds, and then glance at Specks…

Noggin places his hand on my thigh and squeezes it. There's no intimacy in this squeeze, just a statement and a question; thank fuck you woke up, and, what do we do now?

*

I vividly remember the day Specks opened up to me about the domestic violence in his house.

At the time I was a bit pissed off at Noggin, because he had met this wee bird from another school. Like most things that irk us in life, it's not the direct incident but the side effects. I wasn't bothered about him having yet another girlfriend, but, like always, this took some of his attention away from me. She went to Mary Erskine's and obviously thought Noggin was respectable.

I was annoyed because I always had to cover for him every time he met someone or was involved in something he didn't want Jimmy to know about: illness, a Gran dying, away to visit a cousin in Glasgow; the kind of surreptitious excuse Jimmy found plausible.

However, something felt different that day. I wasn't entirely sure I was going to cover for him on this occasion. He *was* my best mate, no doubt about that, but I thought it was time I taught him a lesson about friendship and taking advantage of someone's good nature. Also, what did it really say about our friendship that he expected me to cover for him all the time? What about me? Don't I have places to be, people to see?

Besides, Jimmy had told us the night before that he wanted to 'tan a shed', and I didn't like this one bit.

The shed was in the Burns garden and Goags Burns was someone I liked from School. He got called Burnsy and was one of the more popular guys on the football team.

It was the same drill as 'tannin a hoose', so Jimmy would be furious if Noggin wasn't there. He needs his lookout soldiers.

All of these fragmented emotions were racing through my head as Specks and I stood waiting at a bus stop for Jimmy and Specks suddenly said, 'A'm sick eh ma dad always hittin ma mum and A'm gonnae dae somethin aboot it.'

Amazing how much emotional weight a few words can carry. There should have been a plaque drilled into the bus stop. In about fifteen words he'd told me something extremely poignant about his personal life and also given me a real insight into what he imagined would be his future.

What could I reply to that?

I also wasn't exactly sure if I wanted to be an accessory to this type of information. This outburst from him could have severe implications for the future of his family, and I'm the one he confided in: the one who knew it was going to happen, but did nothing. It's not like I was going to contact social services, or ring the police with what I claimed was just a brilliant piece of prescience, when they would just answer that teenagers say this type of thing all the time.

But Specks didn't, and this was what worried me.

What would I say to him, twenty years wiser? Would I tell him that things wouldn't always be the same? Considering what I witnessed at his funeral, this would have been a lie.

He had his back to me and was spitting on the floor, swirling the saliva about with a small stick. Thankfully there was no one else at the bus stop to take in this vulgar moment, and I had almost come to the conclusion that the best advice was no advice, when he turned and looked at me and opened his mouth…but nothing came out.

We had been standing there for forty minutes and it was beginning to look like Jimmy wasn't coming. Maybe he had a buyer already for this 'great bike' Burnsy owned, and they wanted to have a closer look themselves. I wasn't going to speculate, because quite honestly, I didn't actually care. Like house break-ins, we wouldn't profit from it anyway, so I wasn't going to lose any sleep over something that was far more dangerous than profitable.

I began to say, 'how long should we wait fur um?', but what actually came out was 'how….' and then nothing else. I suppose I was nervously aware I hadn't responded to what he said earlier.

A few more minutes crept past and Specks lit up a cigarette, before beginning to fidget. He then punched the back window of the bus stop and muttered, 'fuck it, A'm away up tae ma cousins,' and then strolled off.

I stood at the bus stop for a few minutes on my own, thinking about whether Specks was going to ask his cousin for help with his dad, or whether this potentially arising provocation would never arise at all and I would always be the only person he confided in. Some therapist I turned out to be.

*

Jane felt it was important for the four of us to get together as often as possible, because maintaining close friendships after entering the much maligned topic 'parenthood' can become difficult; so after successfully collaborating with our respective parents, we managed to book a table for four at *Pizza Express*, North Bridge – childless.

A very amicable waitress had just planted a small dish of olives on our table. What a surprise that Noggin – now the more respectable Kevin – would marry someone who ordered olives. I'm not entirely sure why I find this so odd, I guess it's just one of these things I've always associated with the upper classes and also Jane jokingly said to me on the way here, 'I wonder if Susan will order an Intro...'

The cordial, red-headed waitress had slightly overstayed her welcome, telling us she normally worked in the Fort Kinnaird store, but was just covering for someone today. She then proceeded to tell us how she was studying to be a veterinary nurse, and how she was given the disgusting task of defrosting an already frozen euthanized dog.

This elicited a bit of a gasp from Susan.

After the girl left, Kevin said, 'you're such a snob, Susan. The girl was just being nice.' Not the best start.

We were sitting in one of the comfortable booths, and like always, the conversation strayed from a four-way chat about the terrorist attacks in Paris to Kevin and me talking about football and the females collectively moaning about the incompetence of some nursery teacher or other, when Kevin suddenly leaned in and whispered, 'she's fucking pregnant again.'

'Again!?'

'What kind of reaction is that?'

'Sorry...I mean...congratulations.'

'Ye, ye, very funny.'

'Seriously...that's great news. How far is she?'

'Don't ask that question as if you genuinely care about the answer.'

'Ye, true. Three children, all under seven. That's you fucked mate.'

This produces a wry smile from Kevin, who is looking across the table at Susan looking at us. Of the entire whispered conversation, it's likely the only audible part of it was my *AGAIN!?*

After Susan goes back to her conversation with Jane, I say to Kevin, 'I was thinking about something the other day – something from when we were younger.'

'Right...?'

'Well, remember how I used to cover for you all the time? I don't think I've ever told you about the time I

Jimmy this, Jimmy that

was at a bus stop with Specks and had decided not to do it anymore.'

'Not to do what anymore?'

'Cover for you...'

'What would you have done then?'

'I'm not sure exactly.'

'And you're telling me this why?'

'I just thought you should know.'

Kevin doesn't say anything for a second, and then mutters, 'that's a bit fucking heartless. Just because you led a boring life.'

'Maybe you shouldn't have always – '

'You were obviously jealous...do you know what could have happened to me if you didn't?'

'It doesn't really matter. He didn't turn up that day, anyway.'

'Why are you telling me then?'

'Are you boys having a domestic?' Jane says.

'No...Kevin was just telling me it was his time of the month.'

Jane smiles, and then looks away anxiously.

Kevin picks up his glass and puts it in front of his mouth, before lowering his voice and saying, 'do me a favour. If you ever remember anything like that again, keep it to your fucking self.'

Jane is showing Susan a picture of Luke. She catches my enquiring eye and turns her phone in my direction. It's the photograph of him pretending to be Spiderman. I look at his innocent and trusting face and wonder – after Susan says, 'he's going to be a heartbreaker,' – what his relationship prospects will be like in the future.

Tiny has started seeing this boy. I'm not sure if they're snogging. He seems quite a spiritual type, but maybe this is what she needs: a bit of guidance from above to reassure her life will go on. Noggin seems happy though, so that's good.

I was analysing his behaviour, trying to work out if his sister had said anything to him about bumping into me the other day and how I'd acted really weird. He didn't seem any different, and even when I said to him, 'A bumped intae Tiny the other day,' he just muttered something derogatory about a completely different subject. Maybe she had told him. Maybe she hadn't. Obviously this guy had just walked into her life at the right time and good on him. It's interesting the people you seem to attract when adversity comes knocking at your door. Maybe that's where the Jehovah's come in. My dad says they mean well, but they always come in the middle of the football, so he tells them to fuck off. Maybe we were meant to be with Jimmy. He could have been sent to us: just walked into our lives like the three wise men. Except Jimmy wasn't wise, he was a fucking idiot.

Tiny's new relationship actually coincided with Noggin ending his with the girl from Mary Erkine's. I remember bumping into Jimmy on our way to buy some football stickers and he said, 'did A see you hangin aboot up Clery wi a bird in a uniform?'

Noggin responded, 'it's finished noo anyway.'

To which Jimmy replied, 'dinnae lit me see ye wi one eh they fuckin snobs again.'

Definitely one of those *who does Jimmy think he is?* moments.

To give credit to Noggin, by saying it was over, he wasn't denying the actuality of the relationship, and at least this showed a modicum of integrity. Jimmy just wanted to get his point across, so that's where it ended. Noggin was a bit cut up about it though. I think he really liked this girl. Maybe that's even why he finished it; funny how emotions work that way...

I look at Kevin, who's letting bruschetta fall from his mouth onto the table, and wonder how long my starter has been sitting untouched. I glance over at Jane, who smiles at me, a comforting sort of smile.

'You still with us, mate?' Kevin says.

'Sorry, ye...'

'We thought that Elderflower cordial had gone to your head.'

I laugh, and then pick up my knife and fork, secretly delighted that Kevin seems to have already forgotten our earlier discussion.

'We've got some news,' Susan says.

Kevin grabs my leg under the table.

'Jane isn't the only one expecting.'

'Aw, that's fantastic!' I blurt out.

Kevin laughs.

'Let's celebrate,' Kevin says.

I raise my hand in the air rather overdramatically. 'Should we get a bottle of Champagne?'

'We can't drink,' Susan condescendingly replies.

'Who said it was for you?'

'Wait a second,' Jane interrupts. 'When did you conceive?'

'You mean, when did Susan and I get down and dirty?' retorts Kevin.

This sparks rather rousing laughter from the entire table, and when the waitress returns to clear away the starters, she seems a bit perplexed at our rambunctious behaviour, embarrassingly stretching to take away an empty bottle of raspberry lemonade.

I look towards the front door and four teenage boys are waiting for a table. I glance across at the two females sitting opposite, both shining with the glow of pregnancy.

9

Jimmy got the wrong end of the stick. Apparently the grass was still on the run, and somehow in amongst all the initial blood, sweat, vengeance and tears, Peebo had managed to get this point across. Granted, Peebo was a major player in the *Garage heist* that resulted in Jimmy's dad getting the jail, but he was just the getaway driver and was only offered £50, so what would he gain from grassing on anyone? The real culprit was a boy called Danny – or, 'that wee fuckin prick Danny' – as Peebo repeatedly referred to him as. Danny was supposed to take the money from the cash register and then jump into the stolen car, but on leaving the vicinity a few grand wealthier, he was overcome by a feeling of gluttony and decided to turn a corner and run off in the opposite direction instead.

Noggin had told me all this the day after, because I was, of course, out for the count, so missed every last detail. He said it all just stopped dead and nobody moved a muscle, whilst Jimmy tried to process this unexpected news. Silence had apparently permeated the flat for much longer than was comfortable, when Peebo's friend just sparked a joint and handed it to Jimmy. Jimmy said cheers, and then sat down. This juxtaposition of emotions was described by Noggin as fascinating but also very bizarre.

Jimmy

Noggin was unsure about certain aspects of the story, because the fluidity of Peebo's account was clouded over by fear for his own life, so most of what he told me didn't make much sense. We were still none the wiser whether Danny was the actual grass or if Peebo was just mad at him for stealing the money, because he hadn't actually directly called Danny a grass; he just said the grass was still on the run and Danny was a prick. The only certainty was that Jimmy's information about Peebo being the grass was obviously unreliable. It's not as though Noggin was going to ask Peebo to repeat his story so he could write it down in his journal.

So we're sitting there, waiting…for what we weren't exactly sure. Specks is silent, having been lifted back into an ordinary sitting position by Peebo – who claimed that him lying on his side was 'freakin um oot,' and 'givin um a bad stone.' A minor consolation for Specks: very minor.

Half of his hair has been shaved off and there's an archipelago of blood on his forehead. His eyes have widened and give off an emotionally stupefied permanence. He doesn't have any shoes on and his ankles are tied to the legs of the chair by what I assume is washing-line wire. A trickle of blood is rolling down his chin, presumably coming from his mouth, but struggling to escape because of the duct tape. A tooth is sitting on the table in proximity with the pliers. Any other injuries are currently inconspicuous, but this doesn't mean they're non-existent, and the skinheads don't seem in any hurry to release him.

Whether they intend to inflict any further damage or not is something both Noggin and I are obviously concerned about, but selfishly were also worried we'll be next. What makes the predicament even more frightening is that nothing is happening: absolutely nothing at all; the three of them are just sitting, spaced out, watching something on the TV.

I try to put things into perspective. At this juncture, neither Noggin nor I are in any immediate danger. On the contrary, it seems the feeling from the opposing couch is that we've happily colluded with this arrangement and might be expected to throw a punch or kick at Specks ourselves. Our perspective doesn't exactly help Specks, but what it does do is give us a chance to think, and then possibly collaborate an escape route, in as subtle a manner as possible.

Feeling an unnatural stiffness in my neck, I instinctively turn towards Noggin again, hoping he'll be on the same page as me. He reciprocates my look and blinks both eyes repeatedly. I look away – thinking this is very weird – but then instantly look back, realising this could be some sort of signal. He repeats the same blinking motion with both his eyes, this time a bit slower. I look at Jimmy and his new friends. It kind of suits him to associate with older guys. His disgusting demeanour merges quite effortlessly into the surroundings.

It doesn't take me long to understand the nature of Noggin's message, because looking at Peebo's friend I see what he's getting at; he's blinking heavily and swaying a little from side to side. Actually, all three of them seem momentarily poised, almost as though the world clock has stopped and everything has frozen. Nobody is speaking, except for the mild mutterings from the TV and as I look towards the ashtray, I notice an untouched joint. This unnatural occurrence suggests a change in direction. From gregarious to unsocial, from alert to inert. Again, I glance at Noggin, who one: puts his finger over his lips, and then two: touches his wrist with another finger, indicating silence…it's only a matter of time.

Five or ten minutes pass, and then Peebo is the first to go. Our distant hope of him choosing a far-off bedroom to sleep in is drowned out by the snoring escaping from his mouth. This could potentially upset proceedings, and Noggin bravely says, 'mate, git tae yer bed.' No one responds. Jimmy looks in his direction but says nothing. Peebo's friend then slovenly rises from the couch and exits – leaving no proper explanation of his intended destination. This just leaves Jimmy. It seems fitting that he should be the last one to fold, because once again the four of us are reunited: this time a perfect picture of our position on the ladder of importance; Specks at the bottom, Jimmy at the top, and me and Noggin perpetually going up and down the levels. However, this is currently being challenged, because glancing over at Noggin and me, Jimmy Stokes is staring into four very different and more resolute eyes. He knows very well what's taken place tonight, and so do we. For the first time in our exertions with Jimmy, we can tell that he's wondering if we'll attack him: whether we've got the bottle to avenge our friend. He's weighing up his options and pondering where our loyalty really lies. There's a modicum of vulnerability in Jimmy. Believe it or not, he's slightly unsure of us. The fact that we're both wide awake must be rather chilling. Maybe this is one of these moments in life when we won't be prudent, but in

Jimmy this, Jimmy that

fact act on impulse and cut his fucking liver out as soon as he closes his eyes.

The seconds creep by and still our eyes lock. The level of intensity has reached farcical proportions and we find ourselves more intimate with Jimmy Stokes than ever before…but still we prevail. Throughout all this we know he's just looking for a sign. Some sort of conformation that we're ok with what took place. I'm also encouragingly aware that our eyes locked together will be creating a soporific effect and mixed in with narcotics, Jimmy won't last another minute or two. I think about speaking but don't dare break the moment. We're winning, and he knows it. For the first time ever, Jimmy Stokes will be forced to back down.

Eventually the moment is disturbed by a snort from Peebo, causing Jimmy to stare at him. This allows me to look at Specks, who is staring at us…eyes not so bulbous anymore. He seems to be smiling at us with his eyes: acknowledgment that we wouldn't dare leave him here all night, and are just waiting for the final person to collapse into dreams of barbarity, before making our move.

Then something strange happens: Noggin leans over and takes the stranded joint from the ashtray, before offering it to Jimmy, who declines. An excellent move from Noggin: a peace offering. Jimmy smiles at this, and this confirmation of neutrality seems to ease his nerves and in turn ease him into darkness…

Now the three of them are out for the count: Jimmy and his two acquaintances, who only yesterday he was threatening to stab; too many cans, too many joints, too much living the high life.

After a mutual confirmation the coast is clear, Noggin slowly rises to his feet and makes for the kitchen, whilst I keep my eye on the couch and sporadically glance over my shoulder at where Peebo's friend went only a matter of minutes before. When he returns holding a giant kitchen knife, for a second I think it's to stab Jimmy, but then realise it's actually for more practical matters. I rise from the couch and proceed to squat beside Specks, before slowly tearing the duct tape from his mouth and silently pleading with him not to shout out in anguish. The blood coming from his gums is not a sight to behold, and I tersely attempt to wipe some of it away using the smooth side of the duct tape. By now Noggin has manually sawed through one of the pieces of wire and is working on the other. I can tell Specks is looking about for his trainers, but he'll just have to accept this isn't a priority. Suddenly I speak.

'A want tae git ma bat.'

Noggin simply replies, 'eh!?'

'A just dinnae trust the world anymare…A'm gawn tae git the bat.'

Noggin looks at me, and then goes back to work.

I tiptoe past the couch and pick up my bat. When I turn round, Specks is free and Noggin is simultaneously trying to get him to his feet and eyeballing me, demanding assistance.

The tightness and subsequent abrasive nature of the wire has created a ring of coagulated blood around his ankles and this seems to be causing Specks a lot of distress. He'll need assistance walking until he gets the feeling back. We don't have time to wait for biological miracles, so collectively grab hold of him.

The three of us are up on our feet. I've got my arm round Specks' waist, and Noggin gets the door. We don't even look behind us to see if our actions have woken anyone. There's no way we're turning back now and on looking at my baseball bat I realise on this occasion I definitely wouldn't hesitate to use it.

Neither of us has even bothered to ask Specks if he's ok, but this is probably because we know he isn't.

*

As we turn several corners, adhering to every sign that says *Obstetrics*, I hold back my laughter at Jane's waddle; apart from her beer belly, she's also been instructed to abstain from emptying her bladder since midnight, because apparently it helps gain a clearer picture of the scan. Today is the halfway point in her gestational period and we're about to find out if it's a boy or a girl. Jane is secretly hoping for a girl, but after enjoying more and more football tutorials with Luke recently, I think I'd prefer another boy.

Only separated by a few yards, we first pass a doctor, and then a duty nurse, and then a cleaner. The cleaners' uniform is a grubby, dark blue, meaning someone as far away as fifty yards can recognise the subordinate; the duty nurse sports a lighter blue overall, a name badge, and walks with the air of someone helpful and needed; the doctor is athletic, moving swiftly from appointment to appointment, carrying a briefcase and a clipboard. He wears no uniform and is therefore not part of a system. He is respected. If the doctor approached you wearing a cleaners' uniform, would you offer him the same reverence?

'I'm desperate for a pee,' Jane says.

'Hopefully we won't have to wait long.'

'We!?'

The exclamation mark before the question mark is a clear sign she's distressed and an even more obvious indication whatever I say will come across as attacking, so I simply place my hand on her back in a sympathetic but slightly patronising manner.

After confirming our attendance at reception, we sit in the waiting room. It looks rather settled and free of any obvious stories to take back to friends. However, overhearing the receptionist monotonously mutter, 'obstetrics, how can I help?' and the duty nurse calling absurd name after absurd name, brings a smile to my face, and although these aren't the most obvious of controversial happenings, sometimes it's the subtle things that are the most poignant: the things we don't know about; perhaps the duty nurse is furious at the incompetence of the student on placement; and the receptionist secretly fantasises about the cordial young doctor called Anthony Lazareth – who for someone so young is overwhelmingly hearty and intelligent; then there's the cleaner who furtively pilfers toilet roll from the staff toilet and hides it in her locker; not to mention the rotund girl sitting opposite us who possibly hasn't yet decided if the father is Stevie or actually could be her cousin Davie; then there's the security guard, who probably prefers working nightshift, so he can continue his affair with the night duty midwife called Anna.

As I circumnavigate the clinic, the susurrations of life shout out to me and I smile – a soft, inner smile.

'Speak to me,' Jane says.

'About what?'

'Anything!' she snaps. 'Anything that will stop me pissing all over the floor.'

Two exclamation marks in the space of a few minutes. They really didn't think about the male during this brilliant discovery that holding pee in is necessary, did they? 'You still want a boy?' she adds.

'You still want a girl?'

For some reason this exchange feels a bit closer to confrontation than is comfortable, and after a pause, I say, 'we'll soon find out.'

'We will...' she replies, her voice almost disappearing towards the end of the 'will', indicating no further comment...

'It might be a hermaphrodite,' I spit out, laughing to myself.

The girl opposite looks at me then holds her gaze. Actions speak louder than words and the fact that Jane hasn't replied either speaks for itself.

Our second name is shouted out and Jane stands. I glance at the girl opposite, who is looking at Jane's figure, trying to ascertain if she's in better shape or not. I want to shout at her and say, 'at least I know I'm the dad,' but instead turn my head, place my hand on Jane's lower back and help her move towards the requisite room.

Trussed on the bed, Jane's protruding bump is bigger than it was in her first pregnancy at this point, and I

Jimmy

nervously say, 'there must be about six kids in there,' which earns me a vindictive look from Margot.

I'm just trying to ease the tension, and what kind of name is Margot anyway?

She covers patches of Jane's stomach with cream, before placing the scanner on the bump and moving it about. This magnified creature appears on the monitor, giving off the vibe it's unwilling to stay incarcerated for another twenty weeks. A tear rolls down Jane's cheek. This produces a warm smile from Margot, who I've decided I don't like. She reminds me of Donna, the midwife we had visiting our house immediately after having Luke – who was a sexist pig. Her passive aggressive comments really riled me; 'when he's still in bed from being out drinking,' and, 'when you're breast feeding and he's watching the football.'

I glare at Margot, who seems to be looking at me a little nervously.

'The amount of amniotic fluid surrounding the foetus is the most accurate indication of whether he's likely to be born with Downs Syndrome or not.'

Wait, she slipped up; she said he. Did Jane notice that? I look at her but her expression hasn't changed. You fucking amateur, Margot.

'His hands…which will currently only be about two inches in circumference.'

She did it again. Again I look at Jane, and again, she doesn't flinch.

'The head.'

Better Margot, better; keep it professional.

'Ears, eyes, nose, and mouth. As I move down across the stomach, to the left you'll notice a movement of the arm. As the weeks go by, you'll start to feel kicking and punching. This is very natural and actually a healthy sign.'

'This isn't my first,' says Jane.

That's right, Margot. Don't try and patronise my other half. She knows what's going on.

'Now, of course, as we move down the thighs and have a look at the two feet, there's one area I haven't yet covered. We try and respect a couples wishes on this matter, unless you're happy to know the sex?'

You've said he and his already. I'm so desperate to say this, but Jane looks at me and smiles. She then puts her hand on my leg and says, 'we're happy to find out, Margot.'

Don't start calling her 'Margot', as if she's coming for lunch tomorrow, because she's not.

'Ok…here we go…the little wiggly thing attached to two small peas would indicate it's a boy.'

'Oh my god, it's a boy. I thought it was a girl,' I sarcastically say.

I wonder if Margot was aware of her error and secretly hates my sarcastic announcement.

I try for another joke. 'Is little wiggly thing attached to two small peas the medical name for this part of the body?'

Margot laughs, and then Jane joins in. Suddenly we're all laughing. It seems I've created harmony with my subtle questioning of Margot's credentials.

'This little wiggly thing is going to be a baby boy,' she says.

'A feisty one by the look of it,' says Jane.

I look at the screen, and the baby is moving excitedly – possibly laughing at my joke.

'Not just any baby boy, Margot,' I say, wondering if she could tell by my previous demeanour I was judging her, and hoping that if she did, she'll forgive me and pass it off as mere nervousness about the outcome – 'This is little Gavin.'

this

10

Not only is Kevin driving, he's also just stopping by on his way to pick up little Terry from nursery, so the usual bottle of Corona is being substituted for a strong Colombian coffee with two sugars. He jokingly says, 'you better make it three sugars; two for the existing children and one for the imminent arrival.'

After placing the hot drinks on the table, I notice Kevin has this wry smile on his face.

'I found something yesterday,' he says.
'A fourth positive pregnancy test?'
'Something intriguing.'
'Sounds a bit suspicious…'
'A treasure chest.'
'Like in *Pirates of the Caribbean*?'
'Have you been watching that with Luke?'
'Ye…'
'Is it not a 12?'
'Ye…don't tell Jane.'

Kevin smiles and then looks at his watch. 'I've got his fucking school report.'

'Whose?'
'Jimmy's.'
'I don't understand.'

'I found it in a box in the cupboard.'

A flashback of me finding the baseball bat flies through my head and I smile at the image of my friend Kevin experiencing the same kind of nostalgia. Or maybe vertigo would be a more accurate word?

'How the fuck do you have that?'

Kevin glances down at his coffee, and then slowly swirls the remaining fluid in an anti-clockwise motion, intentionally prolonging this exciting revelation.

'It took a bit of soul searching to remember, but fortunately when I was in ASDA last night, the shape of a courgette reminded me.'

'I could refer to the sexual connotations, but – '

'You're supposed to be a responsible parent –'

'Did someone in ASDA threaten you with a courgette?'

'Very funny…I was in that small fruit and veg shop – the one just across the road from us – and Specks was looking for something to stick in Mr Drummond's drawer as a practical joke.'

'That was very mature of him.'

'Because my mum was never out this shop, I was really paranoid that Specks was going to steal the courgette, so offered to pay for it. He could possibly sense this in me, so in exchange told me he'd give me something interesting he'd found lying on the street.'

'Here was me thinking Jimmy needed it for his PHD application.'

'It's absolutely hilarious.'

'Can I see it?'

'Only if you go to the shops and buy me a courgette.'

this

I smile, but only fractionally, because the thought of reading the school report of Jimmy Stokes is so exciting that any alternative actions or words will really test my patience.

'Have you read it?'

'Only about a million times.'

Kevin then pulls from his pocket something that could almost be a parchment. The paper is not white, but yellow. When he gives me it, it feels crispy – like it could easily crumble with the slightest movement. It's amazing to think even paper has changed over the years; become more mass produced and less meaningful; less personal and more disposable. Kevin is staring into my eyes because he recognises the significance of the moment. He understands and appreciates the feeling I'll get when I open up the first page and it says **NAME**: *JIMMY WALTER STOKES.* Up until now I'd wondered if it was a joke: a fabrication of some sort. All I have is memories and a baseball bat, but the past can be unpredictable, unreliable and inconsistent; it can take on a world of its own. Who's to say Jimmy even existed?

But this is real. This is tangible, concrete evidence that he existed. This is actually the school report of one Jimmy Walter Stokes.

'*Walter?*'

'How brilliant is that? No wonder he kept it to himself.'

'But you moved house a few years ago. How have you just found this now?'

'I obviously just assumed it was one of my own and never actually opened it.'

I begin to turn the pages and stop...because this is more significant than finding the baseball bat. This is proof that it really happened: that all of it was real; every part of it.

Kevin stands. 'I need to water the plants...enjoy.'

He exits towards the bathroom as I close the report again, just to ensure the name on the front is still the same. This is priceless. This is like Anne Frank's diary or gaining access to the president's book. It's like finding the original manuscript of *War and Peace* or actually being able to touch the declaration of independence. In fact, it's bigger than all these things; it's Jimmy Walter Stokes' school report.

Kevin returns.

'You've not even opened it yet?'

'Don't know if I want to.'

'Don't get all sentimental.'

I turn the first page over and can almost smell his presence.

Geography:

When actually present, Jimmy has an adverse effect on the rest of the class. His hostility towards others and complete lack of respect for the subject is very concerning and his failure to complete several aspects of the syllabus has left him way behind. Whether he has the attitude or the capability to complete these before the prelim, is something that only he can decide; a difficult student at the best of times.

Nae cunt cares aboot Brazil or India ya dingal

My eye level moves towards Kevin.

'Wait a second...'

'That's right mate, he commented on them.'

'All of them?'

'Every last one...'

this

Art:
Jimmy doesn't often attend this subject, but when he does, he shows a fair amount of aptitude for originality.

'What!?'
'I bet you weren't expecting that.'
'He was in our class that year, though. Used to throw stuff at the teacher.'
'Might have secretly been a Rembrandt.'

Unfortunately, however, Mr Stokes spends far too much of his time orchestrating disruptive activities amongst other students. It's a shame…he has potential.
A've goat potential wi yer fuckin wife

'Jimmy Stokes and the word *potential* in the same sentence? This is a historic moment.'
'Apparently so…'
'He didn't take it very well.'
'Maybe he thought it was meant as a criticism.'
'In some ways it was.'
'True.'

English:
Jimmy Stokes is a vile student.

'Are teachers even allowed to say that?'
'Just read on…'

Jimmy this, Jimmy that

His adjectives are offensive. His behaviour is unacceptable and the fact he describes Shakespeare as a c**t tells you all you need to know about his attitude in this class. English is definitely not his forte. The only saving grace is that he very rarely attends.

A'm gonnae fuckin kill you bitch

'Very harsh,' I say.
'Is it?'
'Did she not leave?'
'Jimmy probably killed her.'
I laugh, and then turn over the next page.

Religious Education:
Unfortunately I've never had the pleasure of meeting the legendary Jimmy Stokes. He's never attended this class. It's a shame: he obviously can't appreciate the importance of religion.

Jesus hud a small cock and yer ma was the virgin Mary

Physical Education:
It's a shame Jimmy doesn't attend this class more often. He showed great promise in swimming, and although he was too proud to play badminton, showed some dexterity when finally talked into picking up the racket. A bit of a wasted year for Jimmy Stokes so far; mainly due to lack of attendance, but mostly down to attitude.

A only liked swimin so A could stare at the arses ya diddy cunt

'He was pretty entertaining in the changing rooms, when we had swimming.'

'Not for the females…'

As I'm about to turn the next page, Kevin looks at his watch again, and says, 'I better get up to the nursery.'

'I'm not finished yet!'

'You can hold onto it.'

I close the school report and stand. 'Is it too pathetic of me to say this is a beautiful moment?' Kevin laughs. 'We should do this more often.'

'I want that back.'

'Don't get all possessive of Jimmy Stokes.'

'Don't forget Walter…and don't let Luke near it.'

'I won't. I think we should publish it.'

Kevin laughs again, before struggling with his jacket.

I walk him to the door, melodramatically lifting the report to my nose and smelling its further literary potential, before shaking his hand.

After delicately placing the report on the table, I move towards the window and look out. Kevin is getting into his car. He just bought a new *Audi* and I can almost see his reflection off the finely polished metal. Possibly sensing my presence he turns and waves, pulling a very unattractive face – a habit of his that's never failed to make me smile. As I lift my hand to wave back, I look past him at the stretch of grass across the road. There are quite a few teenagers standing about, looking a bit menacing. As I focus on them, I start to consider the poignancy surrounding Kevin's visit and this incredible moment we just shared.

Is it possible: did Jimmy Stokes really have an aptitude for art?

Jimmy

11

All of a sudden we were less confined to the one entity: the entity that was Jimmy Stokes.

We still tried to organise mischievous things, but obviously not on the same barbaric level. We generally struggled to come up with anything promising, and when faced with the monotonous existence of being an ordinary teenager, we felt a bit lost, a little bit inadequate.

One day whilst trying, and failing, to talk this man into buying us some cider, we came across these two street workers.

Fred and Daniel aren't here to patronise us, but give us opportunities people from our area don't usually get.

Like sailing at South Queensferry sailing club.

When we arrive, Daniel extracts this huge hamper from the back of the van. Says it's a kilo of cocaine, but we know it's only sandwiches and juice.

Daniel is definitely the nicer of the two. More laid back, whereas Fred is constantly subtly reminding Daniel they are supposed to be working. This is evident when Daniel says to the guy behind the desk, 'these three have just escaped from prison, so we thought we'd help them over the water,' eliciting a strange look from Fred. A 'remember the boundaries' look.

Jimmy this, Jimmy that

After we secured our lifejackets, a tall guy with dreadlocks shows us to our boat. On the way down the bumpy pier, Specks keeps looking over his shoulder. There is only one possible reason for this: when he said he was going to use the public toilet, he had in fact been feeding his kleptomania habit and nipped into the **SPAR** shop for a steal. Either that, or he was wondering when Jimmy was going to turn up.

The guy with the dreadlocks goes through the drills with us, and most importantly what the three small accessories are on the jacket; a light that works in water; a whistle; and a small plastic hose that runs inside the lining, which you can blow on to inflate the jacket.

All three of us are happy that we don't have an instructor on our boat. Daniel says this is because Fred has a *Sailing License*, and Fred says, 'It's just like a driving license, except we get to go under the bridge instead of over it.'

Daniel thinks this is hilarious. We don't.

The wind at sea is so different from on land, and you don't recognise how helpful buildings and trees actually are until you're out there in the open, with nothing to appease its angry whistles. My nose is running and my fingers are like ice, but I'm having the time of my life.

Is this what guys of our age do that don't have a Jimmy Stokes?

Fred and Daniel are only a metre or so away from us, but we can't hear a word they're saying because of the wind. Then Daniel shouts something into Specks' ear and then almost falls into the water in laughter at his response.

After we stop under the bridge for a biscuit and a drink, I ask Daniel what was so funny, and he says, 'I

Jimmy

asked him if he wanted to stop for a cup of tea, and he said tea's shite, don't we have any coke?', again eliciting laughter from Fred. Again, though, we don't think this is funny.

Obviously there is something about us that they think is hilarious. But all teenagers think adults are weird, so the feeling is mutual.

After half a packet of digestive biscuits and three cans of irn bru, we set off again – but not before Fred explains to us that we will only travel as far as the rail bridge and then go back to the harbour, because reception had warned them of extreme conditions by a certain time, and so our intended trip over to Fife would have to wait for another day. Obviously we were disappointed about only being in the water for an hour or two, but on hearing Fred say 'another day', Noggin's face lit up. Imagine floating in the water on a day when the wind has gone missing. We'd take this over Peebo's flat and 'tanning hooses' any day of the week.

It might not look like it, but we must be about half a mile away from dry land and on circulating under the rail bridge, Daniel points out some precarious looking flotsam climbing up one of the metal pillars. He says it's the dead people who've drowned floating up from the sea-bed to haunt us. Again, Fred gives him the look.

During our about turn, Noggin and I have to lean backwards out of the boat to stop it from capsizing. This is a really enjoyable experience – similar to driving along the motorway at high speed and sticking your head out the window. At the same time we're both trying to tickle each other, twisting and turning, our limbs akimbo, and from

Jimmy this, Jimmy that

a panoramic point of view it would look like two worms wriggling about. We also laugh out loud, because Fred then comments on how this particular sailing manoeuvre must be really difficult for Dave – who we recently found out was the name of the guy with the dreadlocks. What makes this even more enjoyable is the two safety harnesses on the inside of the boat. These are attached to your feet, so that even if you do lean back too far, you won't actually fall into the water. This allows you to be very risky and on occasion let your head ski over the waves.

Unfortunately, this tranquil moment only actually lasts about two or three minutes, before we simultaneously lift our bodies back into the boat. On unstrapping the harness on one of my feet, I look over at Specks. He has a cigarette in one of his hands – which aided by the wind is burning down very quickly – but is neither smoking it nor paying attention to anything surrounding him. Fred is pointing to something far off and Daniel is clapping his hands with joy.

Specks seems to be thinking about something, his eyes fixed on the water beyond us; and as I look at him, I see pain and anguish coming from his eyes and can't help but wonder if he's thinking about life, and how this should be a moment to saviour. Out in the ocean with nothing to fear, nothing to worry about, and surrounded by people who have his best interests at heart.

As the seconds tick by and I continue to analyse his countenance, I begin to wonder if he's thinking about Jimmy. Obviously he's never opened up about that night in Peebo's. Apart from a few missing teeth, there doesn't seem to be any long term effects. Nothing visible anyway.

Jimmy

He catches my eye and holds my glare for longer than is comfortable. He then smiles and perfectly confirms everything I've been pondering, saying, 'that cunt probly would eh chucked eez in the water.'

I look over at Noggin, who smiles at me, warmly, as if sharing my strange nostalgia for Jimmy Stokes. I look at Specks again; distant, like a messenger harbouring perilous news. I want to say to him that this is our new life, and we must learn to adapt. We're ordinary teenagers. We should be grateful.

But something inside me can relate to his thoughts. Something inside me wishes Jimmy was with us on this boat.

We're about fifty metres away from shore, and Fred is telling us in his most authoritarian manner how parental consent will definitely be needed for next week's camping trip. I've never been camping before, and the thought of disposable barbecues, secret bottles of cider, and running about the woods in the night fills me with joy, when something in the distance suddenly catches my eye…

On arriving back at the harbour, there's a lady around fifty or fifty five standing talking to another man with a bowler hat. She's pointing at our boat, and it doesn't seem to be in that amiable way a tourist does when noticing a freight ship carrying goods over the water. It was accusatory, and as we walked up the pier, the two of them slowly descended towards us. The following ensued:

The older lady just happened to be the shop assistant and just like I earlier suspected, Specks had fed his habit before climbing aboard. The woman said out of respect for the club and its members, she'd decided to ask the landlord of the pub across the road to escort her here, instead of phoning the police. She was positive that the grubby looking one – as she referred to Specks – had stolen something from her shop. The pub landlord, taking off his hat and unceremoniously grabbing Specks, proceeded to search him. The fact that Specks didn't argue his case was ominous, and when a rather expensive looking miniature forth rail bridge was extracted, I knew the accusation was valid. However, that wasn't the only item; he had also stolen a key ring with *MUM* written on it, and I couldn't help feeling slightly touched by this.

There was a very long, tense, conversation between the older lady, the Landlord, and Fred and Daniel.

The homeward journey in the van couldn't have been more different even if it was staged. There weren't any jokes. I didn't smoke a cigarette out the window, and Daniel didn't tease us about our lack of knowledge on certain subjects. He said only one thing. 'We both feel a bit disrespected, considering…'

It was the 'considering' part that hurt most. I think it was only because of their kind nature we weren't left to get the bus home. We never saw them again. Noggin and I were livid.

12

Our local chippy sells the best fish supper in Scotland. Enough batter to give you a heart attack, and enough sauce on the chips to replicate the fable about the drowning potato – if such a fable exists. We call it the *Fucking Slippery Slupper*.

The owner Dean, who looks like he eats more fish suppers than he actually sells, is more than happy to give us more batter, less fish, more sauce, less chips.

The aforementioned is why Noggin, Specks, and I are congregated outside the premises, waiting for the shutter to go up. We like to get the chips the moment they're released from the deep fat fryer. Piping hot and still smelling of cooking oil.

Once the chips are all finished, I won't go into detail about what happens with the remaining sauce. Let's just say, people driving to work the next morning will falsely accuse a pigeon of depositing its excrement on their windscreen.

It doesn't actually open until 5pm, so after the slow walk back from school, we still have twenty minutes or so to pass. My mum goes out on a Tuesday night, and my dad is a lazy bastard, so she always gives me money to get my tea. Not exactly looking after my health, but at

Jimmy this, Jimmy that

least she's ensuring I don't go without. Where she goes on this mysterious evening is something my dad has never talked about. The last time I asked him, he said, 'Oot wi her mates, pal.' But there was an undercurrent present. Some form of connotation connected to the word 'oot'. A hesitant tone, as if *he* was guilty of something and not *her*.

As a teenager there are many things about your parents you'll never understand.

The chippy is nicely placed in-between two newsagents. The one on the left is run by an Indian guy called Sharif. Used to sell us individual cigarettes for 15p, and can be seen sporadically looking out his window – searching for fuck knows what. Possibly the police, if an older boy just so happens to be buying the kind of alcoholic drink that seems more suited to the younger generation – Hooch, Merrydown, or the dreaded MD 20/20. This is a regular occurrence in our area, because the older person will always be offered something in return; cigarettes or money. This paranoid glance doesn't mean Sharif won't sell it, because business around here isn't exactly booming. He's just trying to pretend he actually cares about the legal implications, so will probably just mutter something like, 'for you?' before putting his hand on his beard and taking up the stance of a man enquiring. This also happens to be the shop Jimmy has previous with, so we tend to avoid it nowadays – sadly disappointing because the other shop doesn't sell individual cigarettes.

The grubby looking establishment on the other side is owned by a grumpy old man called 'Twat John'. We don't actually know if his real name is John, but he looks like Noggin's uncle John – who we all think's a twat. The reason we don't like him is because he's always smoking outside the shop door, glaring, swearing, and shouting at teenagers for making noise. No idea how he pays the rent on the place, because everybody hates him and goes to Sharif's instead.

There's a rumour going about he has a daughter locked in his attic.

I'm standing on the street corner talking to Lizzy.

Lizzy is my neighbour's daughter, who according to Noggin is someone I should have hit a long time ago. 'Ye should be hittin that mate,' he always says. For a guy with Noggin's potential in life, he isn't half shallow with females. Lizzy has been my neighbour for years and we used to share the bath together. Technically I've already seen her lady area. I should be telling this to Noggin. I should say I hit her when I was four, but somehow this sentence sounds wrong on so many levels, and actually I didn't hit her, I just helped her pick up a rubber duck.

Just because I once warned him to stay away from her, doesn't mean I want her for myself. I just have respect for her, that's all.

She's asking me how my mum is doing, but my gaze wanders as I notice a police car creeping along the road. As it slips out of sight I re-focus my attention back on Lizzy, who asks if, 'A wis even listenin?'

'Sorry...aye, she's fine. Oot the night.'
'Where?'
'Nae idea.'
'She no tell ye?'
'Na.'
'That's a bit weird.'

Jimmy this, Jimmy that

'Ma dad winnae tell me either. She does it every week.'
'Mibee she's havin an affair.'

Lizzy then laughs, but I don't. This possibility has never dawned on me before. Has she been telling him its bingo night, when in fact, she's been banging some guy from her work in a hotel room?

'A wis only kiddin.'
'What?'
'It wis a joke.'
'Aye…'
'Ye look like you've seen a ghost. A wis windin ye up. She wouldnae dae that.'
'Aye…A ken.'

But whilst contemplating the possibility of infidelity in my household, it hadn't even resonated with me that Specks was no longer kicking the ball against the shutter. This would normally be because it was no longer down, but on glancing over I could still see the corrugated metal. Noggin is also looking at Specks, and then past him; at him, then past him.

'See ye later,' Lizzy says, a bit despondent.
'What wis that?'
'Nout,' she replies, sauntering off.
'Awright…aye…see ye...'

I recognise Peebo before I recognise Jimmy.

Jimmy has taken the ball from Specks and kicked it over the roof – much to the amusement of his two associates. He then picks up a rock and throws it at the shutter, shouting, 'yer chips are fuckin shite, ya fat cunt.'

'Awright Jimmy,' I say, softly.
'Who wants tae ken?' is the answer.

Jimmy then flicks me in the ear and punches me in-between the legs, before taking up an unorthodox boxing stance and looking at Noggin. You'd think the three of them would be embarrassed to be in our presence, considering…

'What are you wee fannies sayin?' enquires Peebo.

'Nout,' answers Noggin.

My stomach is tempestuous and my ear is aching, but I stand tall nonetheless.

There's a moment where something has to happen. Like a pause in a script, where the director has to choose either a stage direction or to allow the actor to actually pause and take in his surroundings. Is there a director between us? Is somebody going to decide what happens next? This is the first opportunity we've had to confront Jimmy after that night in Peebo's flat, but I doubt any of us have the bottle. I doubt any of us will attempt any form of retribution: mainly because we fear we might end up in that chair ourselves, but also because we've moved on. We have no intention of getting involved in anything particularly untoward – especially not with these three idiots. However, there's an injustice to be answered for, and the person responsible for it has just punched me in the testicles.

'C'moan Jimmy,' Peebo says. 'Lits git up tae Sean's.'

It's interesting, because in all the time Jimmy was a part of my journey, he only ever physically abused me once. This flick of the ear and punch in the privates was supposed to bring about ignominy. It was supposed to leave me helpless: a direct reminder of my place on the social ladder. However, it had the complete opposite effect. From not being directly involved with Jimmy anymore, this incident was just a reminder of whom and what he was; an opportunity to witness it first hand from the perspective of the outsider. For a period of time, we were standing on the other side, watching and laughing as Jimmy dealt this exact same treatment to some other poor bastard. You never quite capture an accurate picture of someone's immorality until you witness it first hand, and this was definitely the day where I gave thanks for the birth of the skinheads. I thanked my lucky stars that my future would lay outside his circle of trust, and in a perverse and controversial sort of way, I thanked the gods in the sky for the incident in Peebo's flat; because without it, we would have been walking in the opposite direction. At this particular juncture, I had a lot to be grateful for.

The fortification surrounding my testicles and left ear might well have been tested, but as the shutter was raised and we walked through the door of the chippy, I felt such an intense feeling of liberation that I paid for all three fish suppers out my own pocket.

13

We call Noggin's uncle Pete *Avunc Pete*, because the dictionary describes the word avuncular as *kind, like an uncle*. Obviously it was Noggin who told me this. I'd never admit to a sin like looking up words in the dictionary. You'd think I would have been flabbergasted when Noggin said the sentence, 'aye mate, A'v goat the latest version eh the Collins English Dictionary', but I wasn't.

There was a period when someone using a big word like avuncular was rewarded with a slap in the face, but after much consideration we felt this game was unfair and fully accepted Noggin's plea of, 'this games bullshit: it's no ma fault you two are thick as shit.' Sensing this injustice, he corrected himself. 'A'm a loat mare intelligent than one eh youse, and just a wee bit mare intelligent than the other.'

The subtlety went unnoticed by Specks, by I appreciated it.

Avunc Pete owned a pub just off the west end called *Scruffy Murphy's*, and when it was announced we were invited for the night, I thought Noggin was winding me up. Fourteen and going to the boozer: it doesn't get any more exciting than that. The feeling I got from answering the ubiquitous Friday afternoon question 'what you up tae the night?' with 'aw, just gawn tae the boozer wi the boys'

Jimmy this, Jimmy that

was electric. I would actually be able to order a pint at the bar, watch the barman pour it and then hand over a five pound note. Even Gill Bennett – who is fucking gorgeous by the way, does a bit of modelling for page three, and isn't even in my year – walked past me and said, 'heard you're going to the pub. Nice one.' When she then proceeded to give me her sex eyes, I almost prematurely ejaculated.

In retrospect this was a very risky thing Pete was doing. Not only were we four years under age, we weren't exactly the quietest of groups – especially when we had a drink in us.

He explained to us the night would be split into two; when we arrived it wouldn't be very busy, so it would be more appropriate if we just sat in a corner and drank lemonade. He would then sporadically bring us a few pints – on the house – but we'd still keep our lemonades close by in case the authorities decided to pay a visit to the establishment. Imagine him putting his entire business on the line for the likes of us.

So here's us three sitting in *Scruffy Murphy's* on a Friday night; underage, under experienced, but full of enthusiasm. We might never have held a pint glass before, but this didn't mean we wouldn't try and fit in. The premises had an interesting ambience, with oak-panelled tables on one side and delicately upholstered booths on the other. It was a million miles away from the park bench, or the bus stop at the roundabout – where cars got pelted with stones in the summer and snowballs in the winter. This was the new world, the adult world, and we fucking loved it.

On entry, Pete had assured us the place would eventually be jumping, but it already looked relatively

Jimmy

busy to us. Observing the contagious enthusiasm of Specks and Noggin, I could tell they were thinking exactly the same as me: if this is the adult world then fuck being a teenager. You could drink from a glass instead of a bottle; there were girls in skirts, and I'm not just talking skirts: I'm talking mini-skirts, and I hate to use the expression *gantin*, but some of these girls were literally *gantin* for it; tits hanging out, throwing back vodka's like water.

There were even hand towels in the toilet. I mean, hand towels, fucking hell. I normally piss in the bushes and don't wipe: just wiggle.

There were bouncers: Cammy and Big Dee; Cammy was a bit older and Big Dee was really scary looking. Their job was to refuse underage clientele and exit anybody off the premises that was 'no longer with us'. We loved this phrase, and for weeks afterwards Noggin would often say to me in Chemistry 'that cunt is no longer with us' – referring to the fact that our science teacher definitely enjoyed a tipple before class.

Still assuming it was a wind-up, you can imagine the elation when Cammy and Big Dee greeted us with handshakes and bemused laughter. Did I mention Pete was a legend?

Situated in one of the booths at the back; jackets off, shirts ironed and facial hair grown as much as our pre-adolescent faces would biologically allow, we're all sitting bobbing our heads back and forward to *Cotton Eye Joe* by *Rednex*, when Noggin – with his eye on a mini skirt – turns to me and says, 'does it git any better than this?'

'Does it fuck,' I reply. And I mean this. I really mean it. I'm like a seven year old on his first trip to the fire station, or a three year old when you present him with his first bike. I mean without stating the fucking obvious, there are signs everywhere saying it's illegal to serve anyone who looks under twenty one. We're lucky if we look twenty one combined. Specks looks like the fourteen year old who broke into your mate's car. In fact, it probably was him.

I'm thinking about the fact we didn't really premeditate an itinerary for the evening, considering we're virgins at this and should probably be setting certain goals or objectives, when Pete approaches us, and says, 'you boys having a good time? Get out there and mingle. Enjoy the high life. You don't want to be stuck in this booth all night.'

'There's nout in here fur Specks tae steal anyway,' Noggin whispers.

I watch Pete shake hands with a regular and pull down the tap. I watch the beer fill up the glass and smile at Pete's kindness. What a guy. The legend that is *Avunc Pete*. Pete fucking Mandella. The Dalai Lama Pete. Pete the fucking suffragette. Just Pete. Mahatma Pete Ghandi.

Being small and obviously underage, Specks can't help being conspicuous as he approaches the bar. The fact that he's wearing his cousin's oversized shirt only accentuates this conspicuousness and Noggin and I watch on with trepidation. His obvious nervousness doesn't help either, and although we gave him a lesson on what to ask for – 'a pint eh Fosters. Remember and ask fur a pint. Only twats order half-pints' – There's a few rowdy boys at the bar who seem to have cottoned onto the fact a toddler is among them, and may look to take full advantage. Looking at the frown on Pete's face, I can tell this is the type of customer he hates; well-built rugby fans, been out most of the day drinking, and now enthusiastically believe there's no one in the pub except themselves. Normally turning up in groups of about nine, they do exude a slightly formidable energy.

There's a small step at the bar, and because Specks decides to stand on this to elevate himself a little, one of the ruggers laughs and says, 'check out the school boy. Not even tall enough to order a pint. Does mummy know you're out at this time?'

Now…the last thing Specks wants to do is mess with the older generation – even if they are complete tossers – so he just looks at the guy and smiles.

'What are you smiling at? I don't have any nappies you can borrow.'

A rousing laughter bellows from his friends and I'm beginning to regret our decision to send Specks up first. I can see him pondering what to do; trying to muster together his limited brain cells and come up with something that won't have severe ramifications on Pete. He's not the most emotionally intelligent person alive, but even Specks can appreciate what Pete has done for us. He looks over to our booth for support and his facial expression leaves us both feeling helpless. Specks hasn't said anything, which is probably the right course of action. The boy, realising there's nothing more to gain from the situation, laughs and turns back to his mates, but I can tell this has crushed Specks and put a dampener on his experience. Maybe he imagined the world being a different place when you aged. Maybe he pictured a heightened maturity and a mutual respect. Maybe he believed he could lose this inferior demeanour he carried about with him; this cloudy pall. Maybe in all his immaturity and lack of integrity, there was something inside him hoping to escape. Maybe this experience tonight would be more significant to him than it would be to us. Maybe this night wasn't about experiencing the night life of a student, but an opportunity to find out whether he would fit in in the real world, and this arsehole could quite easily have crushed that dream.

Specks didn't perk back up until his adversary was unceremoniously thrown out by one of the bouncers. Being Pete's special guests most definitely had its advantages.

After much encouragement, Specks made another visit to the bar, and returning with three pints and a smile on his face, I felt a love for him that wasn't supposed to exist. He was happy now, so we were happy.

When Noggin started arriving with *Sambuca* shots, I knew it was going to be a messy night.

On one of his visits to our booth, Pete explained to us the opportunity to play the toy boy card, and it wasn't until countless females visiting our table started calling us cute, that we realised he wasn't far wrong. They seemed desperate for a lack of experience in the bedroom, or was it someone without baggage? Maybe it was because they could control us; pet us and help us onto the next stage of life.

Bring it on, I thought.

Noggin had told his parents he was staying at my house, and I had told mine I was staying at his, and Specks; well his parents didn't give a shit where he was, so when I glanced at the clock just above the front door and it said almost midnight, I felt a certain pride: almost like I'd broken through a barrier in life. Like I'd defied the logic of growing up and tackled it all at once. Breaking out of this tipsy reverie, I noticed Noggin leaning against the bar, chatting to some slag. When I say this, I actually mean someone who just wants it. Drinks until they can't walk in a straight line and then pounces like a tiger. You don't have to take advantage of this one, because she'll take advantage of you. After exchanging neck kisses, leg touches and hair strokes, the two would-be-lovers come back to the table together and Noggin says, 'this is Jo-Jo.'

Here was me expecting her name to be Abigail or Patricia.

'Awright pal,' I mutter, trying to act casual, but secretly thinking to myself she could do with getting her teeth whitened. Trying to divert my eyes away from her escaping bosom, it occurs to me that this is most definitely one of these situations in life where I should warn Noggin; try and explain to him that this girl probably has chlamydia and he'd be better looking elsewhere. Several things stop me though; it's his business and he's never cared about my female related opinion in the past anyway; he's already started snogging her in front of us, so my lamentation would be futile; we might never get this opportunity again, so maybe I should be doing the same thing; he probably feels like he can get something from this girl, and it could be done with impunity, considering he's recently started seeing Joanna Hope. This and the fact that a shag would make a fitting end to the night.

I look about for potential suitors of my own, but I'm far too inebriated. The atmosphere and the music have pulled me in. I feel like I'm swimming in an ocean of vagina and tits. Everywhere I turn there's flesh, and it's making me dizzy.

'Mate, miny you ad?' I splutter out – hopefully comprehensibly.

'What?' shouts Specks, because the music has been turned up – maybe the post-midnight policy?

'Nout.'

I look at Noggin and this girl and can't quite believe what I see: she's actually going for it under the table and Noggin isn't even embarrassed. Her hand is rocking back and forward like she's frantically changing gear in an unreliable car. Last time something like this happened to me my member looked ten times smaller because of the lack of degrees Celsius. Should I feel annoyed that he's cheating on Joanna Hope?

'Should we no be tryin tae git oot there?' Specks is saying.

'Go fur it mate,' I reply. 'A'm gawn naewhere.'

Specks laughs at this and I notice Noggin reappearing from his carnal experience with Jo-Jo, and smiling at me.

'Mate, ye still wi us?'

'Should A no be asking you the same thing?' smiling with appreciation for his previous erotic incident, even though erotic is too colourful a word for that disaster under the table.

'A'm gawn tae git ma jaycket,' Jo-Jo says, and fumbles out the booth.

Specks is leaning over the edge of the table, completely out his face.

'Dinnae be fuckin spewin oan ma uncles flare,' Noggin says.

Specks raises his head and laughs. He then mutters the first beautiful and poignant sentence I've ever heard coming from that filthy thieving mouth of his. He said, 'mate, A'v hud a lovely time. A truly huv.'

This creates hilarity at the table and when Jo-Jo returns, she seems to be suffering from a slight ambivalence – wondering if we're laughing at her.

'You comin?' she says to Noggin.

'A will be,' Noggin says and winks at me.

I watch Noggin arrogantly wave to Pete, before stopping to shake hands with the bouncers, as if he comes here all the time. What a hand-job under the table can do for a man's confidence…

'It's jist me and you spectacles.'

'Goan call eez Gavin,' he says.

I laugh at this, but not too strongly, because I appreciate he's having one of those moments. There's no way I'm calling him Gavin. He knows that.

A bell is ringing in my head and I'm beginning to wonder if someone spiked my drink, when the barmaid picks up our glasses and says, 'last orders.'

'Dae A git tae order you?' Specks mutters, a last ditch attempt at replicating Noggin's success.

'I can order you a taxi, but I won't be getting in it.'

She collects six or seven empty glasses, smiles at me, and then moves back to the bar. Pete will have told her about us, so I've no doubt there was nothing in this smile. I can hardly speak anyway, so this confirmation of her cordiality is a reassurance.

'You two are ma only mates.'

Did Specks really just say that?

'Seriously though, if it wisnae fur you's A'd huv…'

I don't think I want to end the night like this. I think we should take up the offer of that taxi.

'You'd huv what?'

'Fuck knows mate. Just furgit it…'

'Fair enough.'

'A'v goat it sorted anyway.'

'Sorted?'

'Fuck aye…'

What has he got sorted? This was definitely one of these moments in life where I should have picked up my jacket…but I didn't. 'Aw, the taxi…did ye phone it already?'

'Naw, ya daft cunt. Mind A told ye aboot ma old man?'

Of course…I won't forget that day, because for the first time in my life I genuinely felt for Specks. Not just in a poor bastard way, but in a brotherly way.

'What dae ye mean you've goat it sorted?'

'Just furgit it mate.'

He's now standing up collecting his jacket, but I'm not finished. He's tickled my conscience. I look into his eyes, and can't work out if he's crying or just really drunk. He was sick in the toilet earlier, but that was a while ago. As he passes me and clambers out of the booth, he suddenly stops, gripping onto the edge of the table, before mumbling, 'ma cousin's dealin wi it. Dinnae tell any cunt.'

Maybe it was the atmosphere that got to him, or maybe it was that after much deliberation Noggin had decided he could come – even though he initially only told me and said he hadn't yet decided on Specks. After the experience with the street workers, Noggin was ambivalent about involving him in anything potentially enjoyable like this, so maybe Specks took this invitation as confirmation of our everlasting friendship. Or maybe he was just feeling a bit older and thought this was what older people did: share their darkest secrets. But what exactly had he just revealed to me? Surely he didn't need to spell it out?

But I wanted him to.

Just a few weeks after this revelation, Specks' dad went missing. I never found out if this was missing with a capital M, or just disappeared. Either dead or gone. Either way, I could only assume the hitting hadn't abated and that someone somewhere had simply decided enough was enough.

14

There's a park we like to hang about in occasionally. During the day it's packed with parents delicately pushing children on swings and dogs peeing.

When the sun goes down, the climbing frames and flying foxes get used for more daring activities, and the age range of visitors narrows. The resplendent red metal holding up the swings slowly morphs into a dark blood red, and a stray dog loiters outside the gate, awaiting permission to enter.

A perfect haven for the likes of us.

The fact it's situated directly adjacent to Peebo's flat is a fine example of the memories one must walk through before getting there. We neither allude to its proximity nor discuss it. We ignore it, because what's in the past is history and history can't be altered.

We're currently outside the park, playing a game of *bottle*. The name of the game is to kick the plastic bottle into the bin from behind the marked line. This game has been made a lot easier because the bin has previously been burned out by bored teenagers like us, so the hole is large. The bottle is filled with a small amount of coke to help with elevation and wind control. There's a tacit agreement we always play a game of *bottle* before entering the park.

Jimmy

There are only three of us playing the game, but actually four corporeal entities present, because Noggin's sister Tiny is out with us today – currently sitting on the park bench, pretending to be engrossed in the game. She's out with us because her mum thought spending a bit of time with Noggin and his friends would help her development. I can only assume she's not referring to her breasts, because they seem to have developed enough already. Obviously we were a bit apprehensive due to knowledge of a certain incident regarding a certain area of her body, but so far she seemed pretty normal. Hadn't said a huge amount yet, but that's to be expected; she's surrounded by three guys who spit, swear, drink and have created the most trivial but fascinating ways of passing time.

Noggin is taking aim and whilst I stand in the queue waiting for my shot, I glance over at Tiny. The pious fucker had given her the chuck a few days ago. Religion might have been her salvation initially, but once she saw through how condescending it all actually is, he probably got bored of her.

I look at her long hair, flickering in the wind – perfectly tinted with a hint of blond – and at her slim legs. My glance circulates the different features on her face and my eyes rest on her hairline. She must sense this, and glances at me. I look away and when I eventually look back she smiles. She blushes slightly when I catch her eye, and then looks away. There's a kindness and vulnerability in this blush.

Noggin misses the bin by an inch or two and Specks lets out a gasp. I'm next up and go for a two pointer – putting a hand over one of your eyes. As I dig my foot into the concrete, the bottle lifts effortlessly into the air – the

Jimmy this, Jimmy that

weight at the bottom dragging it down, defying the laws of gravity. Specks jumps onto the bench beside Tiny and squats, just as the bottle deposits perfectly into the bin. I throw my hands in the air and imitate the commentator of Italian football, 'GOOOOOOOOOLLLLLLLLLLLL, LAZIIIIOOOOOOO!'

I look over at Tiny, who laughs for the first time tonight and this laughter fills my heart with joy.

The importance of scoring the winning goal at *bottle* is not to be underestimated. It gives you privileges; first choice of swing when we play *swingy,* last when we play *stone the footballer,* and most significantly, first drink of the vodka and coke concoction.

The half-litre bottle of vodka is mixed into a 2ltr bottle of coke and passed around the group. I got to start off the drinking – initially avoiding the saliva and crisp floaters – and then passed it onto Tiny. She didn't take a huge amount before passing it to Noggin. Once Specks had it, we would enter the park and head straight for the swings.

The game is very simple: swing and swing and swing until you gain maximum altitude, and then at the perfect moment jump off and attempt to travel as far through the air as possible. When it's not his shot, Noggin will be the designated marker, because Specks is a cheating bastard. We each get three shots and the swing seems to get rustier, louder and less trustworthy with every attempt – hence the advantage of me going first. Noggin's world record is still marked into the ground and I'm desperate to beat it – mostly to impress Tiny but mainly because I'm really competitive. Of course, there's another reason we play this game directly after drinking the vodka, and I don't think you need to be a rocket scientist to work this out.

I post a pretty decent first jump, but, sadly, nowhere near Noggin's world record. I sometimes look at it and think he must have been assisted mid-air by a travelling flock of seagulls to have jumped that far.

Next up is Tiny and she has this suspicious grin on her face. This could be a mixture of alcohol and embarrassment that she's actually getting involved in one of our games. Or maybe she knows something about physics we don't.

As the swing begins to rock back and forward with more and more vigour, I catch her looking at me and giggling; I'm starting to wonder if she might be an Olympic champion when I notice her already in mid-flight. I turn my head quickly and catch a glimpse of her arse. But these perfectly formed bum cheeks don't seem to be getting any lower. In fact, unless the vodka has really gone to my head, they seem to be rising. It feels like time has stood still and we're witnessing something miraculous. I look at the ground and wait for contact. I look past Noggin's world record and outside the park. I look onto the field and down the road. I picture her flying above my house and looking into my chimney. I think of the noise a plane makes and how amazing it was when we went to Germany. I think of water: of warm water and that feeling when you first lower yourself into the bath. I think of masturbating and how it's become a huge part of my life. I think about climax and start trying to form an image of this in my head. I think of all these things and they flash through me in an instant.

Then Specks is screaming, he's shouting, he's dancing about. He's repeating, 'ya fucking beauty,' and Tiny is lying on the floor, frozen in the doggy-style position, reluctant to move her feet. I struggle to comprehend my surroundings as I look at Noggin. He looks away from me in disgust, but must secretly be delighted it's still in the family. Tiny has beaten his world record by an inch or two, and there can be no argument. He could argue the wind was on her side but this isn't the fucking Olympics. He could argue she's lighter, but that would be petty. He could say she's suppler than him from her gymnastics classes, but who uses a fucking word like supple in any argument?

She gets to her feet and runs over and hugs me. Maybe the confidence comes from the vodka, but I embrace her like a long lost family member anyway and then let go. It's interesting; having a female in the group has definitely changed the dynamic. It's almost as though we're maturing and Tiny is teaching us aspects of behaviour we never knew existed. As she pulls away from me I look into her eyes and mutter, 'well done.'

'Wis that a bit eh un-macho-man praise?' she says.

'Eh…aye…ye did…eh…good.'

She laughs and turns away, taunting her brother. It's only taken a matter of minutes, but she feels part of us. She feels like the gap filler, the one sent from above to guide us through this transitional period, whilst we try and shake of the remnants of Jimmy Stokes.

We move over to the spider web climbing frame.

This is a slightly more barbaric game and Tiny incredulously laughs when we tell her the rules: one person climbs up to the top but balances their feet on the third piece of rope down. They are then asked a question. This question is always football related. If they answer the question correctly, they move their feet up to the second last rope without any punishment. However, if they answer incorrectly, every other player involved is allowed to throw a stone at them and they have to take it like a statue. Although the stones are never very big, any facial contact can be really sore. The aim of the game is to get to the top, and then you've successfully made it out of the firing line; however, if you move or flinch when someone is throwing a stone at you, it's known as a *shitebag* and the ramifications of a *shitebag* are severe; not only do you get two stones simultaneously thrown at you, the next question is un-football related. So believe it or not, it's actually in your best interests to take the pain. The intake of alcohol helps with this, though.

Because he was last at Swingy, Specks is first, and after climbing to the top is instantly asked what Italian team Gabriel Batistuta plays for. There's a disappointing sigh when he says, 'Fiorentina' – which is the correct answer. He's then asked what country Ole Gunnar Solskjaer is from and says, 'Norway': correct again. There's a pause and for some strange reason, Noggin looks at Tiny – who has her arms crossed and is looking a bit sad. 'A cannae be arsed thinkin up the questions,' Noggin says. Specks remonstrates he's only one correct answer away from the finish line, but Noggin just turns his back on him and walks away.

He understands that to invite someone else into the group means you have to adapt to their ways. You can't ostracise them by playing games they don't feel comfortable with. I appreciate for the first time his filial kindness. I accept his subtle lamentations about baby-

Jimmy this, Jimmy that

sitting, but his obvious admiration for Tiny outweighs this. He can see she really enjoyed *swingy,* because it made her feel like an ordinary teenager again, and after all, this is what the purpose of her attendance was in the first place. He can recognise standing on the side-lines, watching on as other people have fun is the last thing she should be doing.

Noggin stops, and then turns back. 'D'yae wantae see the game we invented oan the flying fox Tiny?'

She looks at him and smiles. 'Na…you go ahead.'

'Ye awright?'

'Fine…' she replies, embarrassed at this slightly awkward moment.

He smiles at her and then looks at Specks. 'Specks?'

'Fuckin right,' he answers, and without prior invitation, hands me the bottle of vodka and coke and then runs towards the flying fox.

Leaving me alone with Tiny.

I hand the bottle to her, and then look over at the other side of the park. She swigs from it and I laugh as Noggin is upside down on the flying fox, Specks dragging his feet. It's the first time I've ever seen them interact this way. It doesn't seem forced, but natural. There doesn't seem to be an emotional disparity, but a connection. Noggin's parents are encouraging, Specks' parents are…well, we don't need to go into that. But there's an unforced acceptance between them; cordiality brought on by the presence of Tiny: a belief that we've truly moved on and are ordinary teenagers again.

Tiny passes me the alcohol and says, 'ye dinnae come roond anymare.'

An excruciatingly painful moment goes by.

'Eh…A've been busy.'

'Fuck off,' she mutters. 'A'm no daft.'

And then we have another awkward silence. An understanding materialises between us that I've been cruel. By refusing to go back to Noggin's house, I'm confirming she was raped and doesn't deserve to be normal anymore. She makes me recognise instead of being mature about it, I was childish. I ran from it.

She then laughs and says, 'ye niver spoke tae me anyway,' – obviously attempting to ease the situation.

'A'm yer senior,' I say to her. 'Show eez a bit eh respect.'

Immediately I recognise the rape related connotations connected with what I've just said and feel awful. I realise I must fight this awkward feeling. I must divert it somehow and pretend it never happened. Or better still: stop worrying everything I say might be in some way related, because this doesn't help either. She's just a teenager who was in the wrong place at the wrong time.

'Yer only ma senior in age. Kevin told eez aboot yer Prelim results.'

'Cheeky bastard,' I grin.

And then something happens. A movement occurs, originated from the locking of eyes, and suddenly we move towards each other…and kiss.

A minute or two later she has her tongue down my throat and her hands gripping onto my back. I push her against the fence and we start kissing again. This time she puts her hands around my waist and I put my hand on her face. Girls always close their eyes during kissing, as though they're trying to transcend or practice some tantric Buddhist shit. She's a really good kisser and sticks her hand up my top. Her cold hand on my bare chest only accentuates the intensity of the kissing and for a moment I feel like I'm floating under water. I can taste the alcohol from her breath and somehow we turn around so I'm against the fence and she's looking out into oblivion: the world outside the park. I glance over towards the flying fox and both Noggin and Specks have stopped moving. They're staring in my direction and have become like statues. I'm looking at Noggin for approval. He seems to move forward but maybe it's just the focus of my eyes improving. I look into his eyes and then at his mouth. He smiles, a warm, comforting smile. He seems to be thanking me without speaking. I watch him climb back onto the flying fox and suddenly feel immensely happy. I'm kissing Tiny but my intimate feelings are towards her brother. It might be the drink invading my senses, but I can't help but feel an unequivocal love for my mate Noggin at this time.

I pull away from Tiny and she smiles. The transcendental moment of a kiss is soon drowned out when it finishes. You then have to deal with the consequences of your actions. I take her hand and feel confident enough to publicly hold it. She puts her head on my shoulder and rubs her fingers through my hair – confirming for the moment I'm her man and it was more than just a kiss. I look outside the park at an older woman walking her dog and think to myself: what of Jimmy Stokes?

Because it's suddenly apparent nobody seems to give a shit about him anymore. Tonight it's the four of us, but not the same four. The dynamics couldn't be any more different, and a feeling I haven't felt in a long time materialises. A feeling of perfect satisfaction.

15

We're running an errand for Noggin's mum and have to cut through the graveyard. Sorry, I'll rephrase that: we've decided to cut through the graveyard. People don't choose to walk through graveyards in the dark, because anybody they come across will either be climbing out a grave or looking for the perfect candidate to put in one.

It's difficult to specifically pinpoint exactly why a graveyard is so eerie. It's not the longevity of the stone and how it never crumbles – only fades with years of fighting weather; it's not the significance of the flowers meticulously planted beside a loved one, assuring them they're gone but not forgotten; it's not about the crow perched on the tree or the hooded man with the scythe; it's not about the fact some corpses have been there for many, many years, and our brain can't comprehend the fact that they perpetually repose and never come out to say hallo; it's not about the pure multitude of dead people in such a small area; it's about how so many of these people lived before our generation, and witnessed things you only read about in books; it's about walking past a gravestone and seeing a name you might recognise: a name with significance; it's the fear of walking past a gravestone and seeing your own name.

'Thers a loat eh Anne's eh?'

'No everyone called their bairns coconut and Olive branch.'

'Look at this yin…born March 1977, died May 1977. The cunt wis only two months.'

'Well done,' I whisper. 'Yer good at maths.'

'Why ye whisperin?'

'Probly cos ye referred tae a deed baby as a cunt,' Noggin says, indignantly.

I laugh at this, but then think about what was just said; why was I whispering?

'Worried yer gonnae wake up baby Anne?' Specks says.

'D'ye wattae fuckin stoap that!' bellows Noggin.

'What?'

'Ye ken what!'

'Dae A?'

'Stoap saying derogatory shit aboot deed babies.'

'She died fuckin years ago.'

'Then lit er rest…'

Specks pulls out a cigarette and puts it into his mouth. I usually get Noggin, but sometimes Specks struggles to ascertain the level of his seriousness. I'm not particularly happy about his sacrilegious attitude towards the dead either, but I don't really expect anything different. Noggin takes history very seriously and occasionally condescendingly talks to me about wars and *No man's Land*. I don't think he minds someone talking about death, but he seems to despise when the dead are disrespected – as if they never played their part in society.

'Nixt you'll be fuckin diggin somedi up,' Noggin says.

Specks stays silent, and then lights up his cigarette.

Jimmy this, Jimmy that

As the flame flickers I can't help but feel like I noticed a silhouette palpitating off one of the larger gravestones, but quickly put this down to paranoia.

I'm about to dismiss this notion completely from my thoughts, when Noggin – completely contradicting everything he previously said, but for his own benefit of course – says, 'see Specks, you've woken the fuckin deed noo.'

A mixture of laughter and incredulity passes through me as I notice what looks like two people moving about in the distance.

'If we go roond that wey, we'll see what's gawn oan.'

Creeping closer, we're all praying it's something corporeal and not a floating vampire sucking blood from the neck of an innocent female. As we approach it becomes evident there's flesh on view and that this might be someone attempting to create life in amongst the dead. How horribly creepy does that sound?

'Are they fuckin shaggin?' Specks whispers.

We congregate behind the grave of Dave Hopkins – one of the new recruits, with only three years underground – and as I slide my finger across the marble, I can't help but feel a bond with him. I can't help but wonder why I'm still here and he's not. At only seventeen, young Dave thought he had everything to live for, and now he's stuck in here; three guys surrounding his place of repose, secretly enjoying spying on a couple having sex. I wonder if my stroking will awake Dave. His gravestone might work like a genie in a lamp.

'Should we git a bit closer?'

'Naw, ya fuckin pervert.'

Specks pulls out a slingshot. Is he actually being serious? And why is he carrying it around? In case we bump into the dead?

Or maybe he carries it about with him as some sentimental reminder of Jimmy and his hugely important job during house robberies.

I vividly remember one day approaching Specks' house and seeing him aiming his slingshot at a small ginger cat. I stopped for a minute, wondering if he would be accurate enough, or whether he was just testing the durability of the elastic. I pondered whether I should throw a stone towards the cat, hoping it would run off...but something stopped me. I couldn't help wanting to know if he'd go ahead with it. Not that I thought Specks had any particular love for the animal kingdom, but it would have really upset his neighbour, so he was taking a bit of a risk. When I eventually decided to move closer, I saw the neighbour opening her window and shouting for the cat. I shouted out to Specks, but he didn't answer, and when the relatively big stone was flying through the air I couldn't help notice another cat sitting on a windowsill over the road, looking out for his friend, praying he would survive. Or maybe the cat sitting in the comforts of his home was some sort of feline nemesis and witnessing the downfall of this little ginger fucker would be a pleasure. I wasn't confident about this though, because even from afar I was pretty sure I could see empathy in its eyes. The cat at the window then rose up onto its back legs and started scratching the glass, just as the other feline took a vicious blow to the kidney.

'Fuck it, A'm movin closer,' Specks mutters.

Jimmy this, Jimmy that

Slingshot in hand, he slithers out from behind the gravestone of Dave Hopkins and furtively moves towards another Anne. This time it's Anne Polworth – a retired nurse, who died in 1966. Deciding it unwise to separate, Noggin and I swiftly join him and on arrival Specks says – looking a bit perplexed, 'born in eighteen eighty fuckin two? She wis aboot a hundred.'

'Life seems a bit unfair when ye look aroond here...' Noggin says. 'She wis eighty four when she died, ya dumb prick...'

Now we have a better view of the fornication. In fact, we are so close we can actually hear the moaning and groaning. The sensuality is mesmerising. How these two can innocently lose themselves in a graveyard is beyond me, but there you have it. From our viewpoint we can see a grubby looking pair of buttocks and longish dirty blond hair waving about. His buttocks are pumping back and forward in a perfect rhythmic fashion and the girl is wrapped around him, fists clinging onto his back. There's grunting coming from the male and little bursts of moaning from the female. She's looking in our direction, and although it's highly unlikely, I feel like we lock eyes. I feel like I can read her thoughts and fears.

I'm crouching, thinking about sex, and whether this could be classed as an erotic situation. Would I say two people having sex in a graveyard is erotic? Is it the type of scene you would wank over? Would it make the cut in the pile of porn videos I've got stashed under my bed? It could never cross the barrier from sex to making love, that's for sure; not because it's too cold, too risky, or too uncomfortable, but because it's too impersonal: the list of possibilities is endless. So why are these two enjoying this so much? Maybe it's because of the situation? Maybe it's because they know we're watching? Maybe the thought of pumping away on top of the dead excites them?

'That's fuckin Jimmy,' Specks mutters.

'Naw it's no.'

'A'm tellin ye.'

'Ye mean, ye wish it wis Jimmy.'

I have to confess, it does look a bit like his terrible hairstyle, but this certainly isn't anything to go by because most teenagers of our age get a short, back and sides.

'Ye would ken what his arse looks like, right enough,' says Noggin, but I instantaneously recognise doubt in his face. He looks pale because of the dark, but aided by the flickering light from the lamppost outside the cemetery, I can just make out a reticence in his expression. The even more mysterious thing was the girl. When I felt as though I locked eyes with her, it triggered some sort of recognition. She reminded me of the girl Noggin went home with that night in the pub.

'Fuck um,' Noggin says.

'What if it is um?'

'Then fuck um,' Noggin says again.

Noggin points to a larger gravestone a metre or so away and then signals for us to put up our hoods. After following this instruction, I scramble about in the dark searching for a sizeable enough stone, well aware I could easily pick up dog shit, but willing to take the risk, because this could well turn out to be a momentous occasion. As I pass the stone to Specks, I consolingly mutter, 'ye sure aboot this?'

Jimmy this, Jimmy that

'Fuck um,' Noggin says again, and I smile in appreciation of his repetition, because he's obviously attempting to get Specks in the zone. I look at Specks – who seems to be attempting to use sense memory to transcend back to the successful striking of the cat. This could be Jimmy Stokes, and Specks has an opportunity to violate him both physically and mentally. I'm sure we'd all like this opportunity, but for reasons we don't have to mention, Specks deserves it most of all. There's no chance we'll get caught either, because it's pitch black in here and he won't even know what hit him. This lucky bastard is well on his way to coming and if the stone strikes before climax, he'll possibly wonder if he's having an outer body experience. He'll maybe even contemplate the grave he's balancing against and the name written on the stone. He might think about the significance of the person's prior career and whether he's chosen someone that would disagree with this activity. He'll consider an animal biting him, attacking him. He might even think someone has stabbed him. It's possible he'll accuse the female.

As Specks pulls back the elastic, in preparation for attack, I'm momentarily distracted by thoughts of the errand; it's for Noggin's mum and considering my recent succulent tasting of his sisters tongue, I better ensure we get it completed.

I look at Specks and he's frozen. It doesn't take telepathy to recognise he's bottling it. Against all the odds he still has love for Jimmy Stokes. He's like a female who goes to work with sunglasses on because her husband has given her a black eye, but still returns to the same home again and again. Something about the pain attracts her back; it gives her meaning; being part of the controversy seems to drive her; it's not simply just fear of her assailant, but something much deeper.

Noggin takes the slingshot and the stone, and then looks at Specks. 'Even after…' but then he stops, because the unsaid seems more powerful, weightier. There's not much chance of Specks partaking in a session of personal therapy, so Noggin looks at me and then turns on the victim. For years to come I'll remember this night as the one time Jimmy Stokes was the victim, and being able to use this word on him was a beautiful feeling.

As the stone whizzes through the air, I think about the cat. How, like our target, it was given no prior warning of its downfall. The moment is short-lived, because we hear a whack similar to swatting a fly against a wall, and then a roar of confusion. At once we disperse, ninja like, the three of us quickly forming an audience behind the planned gravestone of Doug McAllister. Watch over us, Doug. This type of act can't be underappreciated. The proverbial bar has definitely been raised. We've embarrassed him on several counts and he's desperate to find out what's going on. However, just as predicted, he doesn't seem very sure if he was attacked or possibly suffered a stroke; he's shouting at the female, asking her if she bit him or kicked him. I can't help but congratulate Noggin by patting him on the back, but he's silent; he looks a bit paranoid. Maybe he didn't actually believe it was Jimmy and now that he's realised it is him, he's suddenly terrified of the ramifications.

Although the copulation has ended, there's not a huge amount of movement, because Jimmy still seems undecided if anything did in fact happen, or if it was all in his imagination. After accusing the dead – much to our amusement – he moves forward slightly, dragging the girl with him. He then stops and seems to be rubbing his side, and thinking he is understandably in pain and just attempting to assuage it, I don't really think about the next part until I see the gleaming, the reflection of the polished silver, and it dawns on me he's carrying a knife.

Producing a lighter, Jimmy takes very small steps, raising the knife every time he hears the rustling of leaves, the movement of a mouse, or the whispering of the wind.

'That better no be you Gammy, ya cunt, playin tricks oan eez!'

I'm desperate to ask who Gammy is, and what he has to offer the world.

He's only a few metres away from us and can possibly hear our heartbeat.

Noggin passes me a stone, which I throw as far as I can over Jimmy's head.

The flame creeps back into the body of his lighter, as he turns with a grunt.

No doubt the girl will be used as a scapegoat for his failure.

16

This is the third week in a row we're skiving religious Education. It's taken a while to organise this trip to Portobello, because Mr 'I'm really particular about the classes I'm willing to miss' has always had some sort of excuse; 'we're workin oan Arthur Millar's *Of Mice and Men*', or, 'A've gottae try and work oot this *Assisi* poem mate: it's a hard yin tae crack'. That was week one and two, but on this particular week, English has been cancelled, so R.E is the only subject we have on a Wednesday; which fortunately Mr Einstein doesn't care about.

The four of us are standing at the school gate, waiting for Tiny. No, the fourth person isn't Jimmy Stokes: it's Joanna Hope; the pair of them now a fully blown couple – 'shagging all over the place' according to Noggin. Information nobody wants to know, but he'll tell us anyway. He can have her…I've got my girl. We might not have done it yet, but that's ok. The right time will arrive…

I'm watching Tiny cross the small stretch of grass, drinking a can of *Tizer* and waving. She's never actually met Joanna before, so I wonder how they'll get on. Hopefully Joanna's not one of those types who has a rule about people from the year below. I'm currently overanalysing the complexities involved in said first meeting, when

Jimmy this, Jimmy that

Noggin says – rather callously, 'so now she's skivin school tae be wi ye.'

Maybe I haven't taken into account certain aspects surrounding the whole brother/sister thing; he did a favour for his mum, which seems to be dragging on for a lifetime; or maybe he quite simply just doesn't want to hang about with his wee sister anymore; or it's perfectly plausible that he's just acting hard in front of Joanna.

Or maybe he doesn't want his sister dating me. I might be his best friend, but the reality is I've got absolutely no ambitions in life, and we all know about Noggin's ambitions; he knows youth is only temporary, and one day we'll all grow up. He prides himself in perfectly managing both elements of life; enjoyment and prudency. Probably preferred the pious fucker over me.

But Noggin's not daft, he knows where he stands in our friendship, and knows how I respond if he oversteps the boundaries – which is why we're still friends now I guess. I know there was no real malice involved in his comment, so by standing back and allowing him and Joanna to get on the bus first, I communicate that there's no hard feelings but just try and be a bit more respectful in future. Amazing how much you can say without actually having to open your mouth.

Tiny and I sit together, holding hands, and just as the driver puts his foot on the accelerator, she kisses me on the lips. Using surreptitious hand movements, I manage to prolong this kiss, just as a kind of fuck you to Noggin, before pulling away and smiling at Joanna. I can tell this slightly disgusts her, which makes me all the more delighted to have done it. She's obviously not one for

Jimmy

public affection, making me wonder if Noggin's amorous stories are actually just a cover up for something which hasn't yet happened.

Specks has brought along a few unopened straws from McDonald's. He must have had some in reserve, because it's a few days since we were last there. We habitually play the *soggies* game on the bus, but I'm not sure if today's environment is appropriate. Try telling this to Specks though; he's not trying to impress anyone, and is already putting a piece of paper in his mouth and preparing to spit it through the straw at some unfortunate person's elegantly ironed shirt. We often play this in school, but buses are better, because they're more crowded and the window of opportunity to pretend you're innocent is wider. Also, you can't get detention if you get caught – only a ticking off from a less than amused commuter.

An older man has turned from his paper and is looking in our direction. He presciently senses mischief – like Sherlock Holmes – and although hasn't been one of the victims, he still doesn't like what's going on. He goes back to his paper without passing comment, but not without looking around for support first. He doesn't get any though, because hardly anyone cares about things that have no direct effect on them.

Specks has now elevated his straw – attempting to fire over everyone's head and hit the person right at the front of the bus. On ripping a larger piece of paper, he begins rolling it about his mouth and mutters, 'watch this.'

The small, round, soggy object leaves his mouth, moves in and out of the straw, before flying through the air at maximum speed and splatting against the window at the very front. The bushy haired woman – who was engrossed in a book and got a bit of a fright – furiously turns round and looks behind her, trying to ascertain the perpetrator, her search being aided by the older guy with the newspaper, who is looking at us again.

Joanna turns round and says, 'that's really immature. How old are you?'

I stifle my laughter, almost asphyxiating myself in the process, just as Tiny grabs onto my other hand and squeezes. I look at her and smile, attempting to hold back the tears.

'Somethin funny?' Noggin says.

'Just eh…'

'Nout,' Tiny says. 'She's right, stoap being immature Specks.'

Joanna looks at Tiny and smiles. This motion of her brings me closer to Tiny. How she precociously managed to level the situation, but in the same breath use the words to her social advantage was brilliant. She balanced being magnanimous with being self-assured; she broke the ice with Joanna in the most perfect fashion imaginable.

As we jumped off the bus on Portobello Road, I wasn't sure how I was feeling. If Joanna wasn't one for joviality, this could cause a slight problem, because we were as immature a group as you'll find.

After meandering around the main street – praying Specks wasn't tempted to steal and enjoying some of the recreational activities in the amusement centre, where we lacked proper enthusiasm for the gambling machines, having tasted the joy of playing the real ones in the pub – we decided to walk down to the beach, where it's usually all happening. When I say all happening, I'm not talking about joggers, aristocrats drinking double espresso's on the outside benches, or even dog walkers; I'm talking about the beach itself. Great stretches of sand, families splashing through the water, kids making sand castles. There's nothing else like it, and the possibilities with sand are endless.

The three of us are playing football, the two females watching from afar.

Specks has created two goal posts using mine and Noggin's jumpers, and we're currently simulating a penalty shootout witnessed on television last night, where the teams kept scoring and scoring and we didn't think it would ever end. You know a game has gone on for ages when the ten o clock news ends up being at eleven. Noggin is running towards the ball and I'm pretending to be a man from the news scratching his head and wondering when he will get to go on air, when I hear a chuckle coming from the girls. I look to my side and notice them both laughing. Joanna has dropped ice cream onto her jumper and Tiny is attempting to wipe it off. This moment of friendship fills me with great joy and I look over at Noggin, but he's looking at Specks instead. And now he's not looking at Specks, but not at the girls either. We've both then settled our eyes on these two approaching men wearing hats; both wearing too many layers for a hot summers day, but passers-by fully appreciate it's just etiquette, uniform and appropriate for their particular line of employment. They have radios, truncheons and pepper spray also. They're intermittently taking off their hats and waving them across their faces like a fan. My instinct is to look at Specks because they're

Jimmy this, Jimmy that

coming this way, so I do. I look along the promenade at all the people and just assume they're here for us. This has nothing to do with the fact they're coming directly towards us, crossing the sand, but because we're in the presence of Britain's most notorious thief. As his Adams apple moves up and down his larynx, I can tell Specks is guilty. Of course he's guilty: he's always fucking guilty.

Tiny and Joanna have stood up, obviously in anticipation of some provocation arising and wondering what the best thing is to do. Specks is going through his pockets – possibly attempting to muster together a plausible enough alibi – whilst our football rolls towards the sea. Noggin is rubbing his hands through his hair and I'm just staring at these two men in uniform coming closer and closer. We hear a description come over one of the radios and what does it say about Specks that I don't even listen to see if it matches his attire?

But I don't have time to think anymore, because they're suddenly right beside us, perfectly still, like two statues looking down upon the townspeople. One of them has ginger hair and is slightly fleshier; the other, who is significantly taller, elevates his head downwards.

'I hope you boys are behaving yourself?' he says, and then laughs at the heavy set one, who starts waddling off to retrieve our ball.

When he comes back, he says, 'there you go boys,' and hands the sand soaked football to Noggin.

They then walk towards the edge of the water and stand, staring out at the open space. Then something incongruous happens; they both take of their police boots and socks and go for a paddle. This strange image seems to draw a bit of a crowd and those around us are laughing and pointing. It's as though these two men are defying their duty as police officers, but in the most extraordinary manner. Even a man walking his dog a hundred yards away has stopped to look. They're fighting like teenagers in the water, splashing each other and having fun. We give people titles and categorize them, but we're all just the same in the end, we all want that feeling of liberation, of laughter…if only for a short time.

A few minutes go by and eventually they come trundling and laughing out the water and sit on the sand. They share a towel to dry their feet and even comically throw sand in each other's eyes.

They start coming in our direction again and for a minute I imagine they had actually just been passing time before administering arrest, when the ginger haired one says, 'what's wrong, never seen a policeman enjoy himself before?'

The five of us stood there for a few minutes, not speaking, just thinking. What we were thinking about I'm not entirely sure, but one thing was certain, Specks had noticed our accusations and didn't say anything on the bus back.

To be honest, I wasn't really that interested in this moral dilemma, because just as we were approaching home, Tiny put her right hand just a matter of inches away from my important parts.

17

The park: again; late enough for darkness to settle and foxes to start roaming the streets, searching for scraps.

This time there's only two of us; me and Tiny. We're snogging, touching, laughing and joking. We even have silent moments, because we're used to being in a group and not alone; the kind of moments where you expect the heavens to open and classical music to come blaring from the sky. This is where we enjoyed our first kiss, so there's a lingering sentiment with every taste of her lips, every finger circulating the smoothness of her back.

A few days ago we had the 'boyfriend' chat. It was really vague and immature, but we eventually reached a conclusion. It was now official we were a couple and I wanted to wear a sign on my head saying, **'*single? No any mare*'**.

Naturally I was delighted, but who wouldn't be with a girl like Tiny; she's smart, personable, respectable, and let's not forget gorgeous. She might not be conventionally attractive, but who wants to follow stereotype anyway? She's the type of girl who can wear anything. Sometimes she comes out with this tartan granddads hat on and I'm looking at her wondering why it suits her so well when it quite obviously shouldn't. The fact that she has the confidence to wear it in this particularly judgemental phase of her life makes me even more attracted to her. She's sophisticated, educated, and sensitive. She's also slightly shy, which is such an attractive attribute because shy people are the most loyal.

Tonight might seem like any other night, but it's not. Last night, whilst I was snogging Tiny goodbye – much to the continued disgust of Noggin – she said, 'mibee we could stey oot a bit later tomorrow: just the two eh us.'

I'm not daft; I know what she was referring to.

It might be at least forty five minutes since Noggin and Specks left, and we might be really enjoying our kissing and touching, our privacy and the feeling of being left alone, but there's also a subtle tension in the air, because I know why we're here, and so does she. There are only so many occasions I can rub the bottom of her back or subtly rest my hand on her breast; she can't continue to rub me from the outside, allowing me to get harder and harder until my joggers almost rip. We're going to have to do it eventually, and she couldn't have put it more plainly. I'm not just talking about finger penetration; I'm talking about a part of my anatomy connecting with hers. I'm not just referring to having intercourse with some slag from the year above; I'm talking about actually having sex with my girlfriend; awkwardly fumbling to get the condom on and searching for that gap in-between her forest. I'm talking about concerning myself with the current climate and hoping it doesn't affect the size of my penis; hoping I can perform to a decent enough standard and making sure she feels relaxed and comforted at the same time. Most importantly, it could be the start of something. If things go well tonight I could end up in a sexual relationship, and regularly doing it.

I spent a lot of time preparing before I left the house tonight; not only did I shower, I also had a bath. I even scrubbed areas I didn't know exist – like the scrotum and that part just on top of the testicle where the penis usually rests. I surreptitiously ensured my mum and dad were together in the kitchen, so I could steal some of his *Yves Saint Laurent* aftershave. When brushing my teeth after my macaroni and cheese, I pedantically inspected my gums and lips in the mirror, just to ensure the remnants were all gone. The hardest part was the condom, because it's not like I was going to ask my mum for it. I had to steal it, and only really knew where to find them because I once rummaged around her drawers looking for money and came across a packet of durex extra. On taking one from the packet the 'extra' part made me feel really nervous, almost as though this type of protection was only for more experienced shaggers, and I'm not sure if I was at that level just yet. I guess I'll soon find out.

Checking myself out before leaving, I couldn't help thinking that of course the preparation counts for nothing if the act itself is a let-down; what if she doesn't like it? What if it's over in ten seconds and she's really disappointed? What if the condom bursts and she gets pregnant? What if I try and stick it in her belly button? What if an alligator comes running over the field and bites my arse? What if God decides this isn't my moment, and seeks retribution for all the times I've contradicted his supposed moral code of what is right and what is wrong? What if I'm actually wrong, and she just wanted to spend some quality time together, getting to know me a bit better? What if I die whilst we're having sex?

But all these aforementioned fears prove unwarranted, because within a matter of seconds she has her hand inside my joggers and is yanking away. Of course the terrifying possibility of ejaculating before we even get to the next stage is becoming more and more of a probability, so I begin to think about my Gran. What a disgustingly revolting thing to admit to, but psychology plays a bit part in climax control, and if the picture of my grans haggard and wrinkly face stops me from embarrassing myself, then I'll deal with admitting to this thought.

Everything is going just as planned and she's even grabbing onto my hand, trying to pull it towards her lady area. I would like to make this a slow process, but she's wearing a skirt, so access is totally undisturbed. As my hand touches flesh and she continues to stroke my member, I begin to think about other people who revolt me; Uncle Teddy has this really disgusting mole on the side of his face that I've often wondered why he never gets surgically removed. You can get these things frozen and cut off. Maybe it's some sort of sick fetish of his wife's. Then there's Miss Fleming, the school nurse, who looks like a cross between a bulldog and a gorilla. But this doesn't seem to be helping much and I can feel my insides squirming as I struggle to hold on. Maybe I should just let go. My suffering is then accentuated when she pulls away from my lips to take a breath, and notices this constipated look on my face; almost like I'm struggling to squeeze out a jobby.

Jimmy this, Jimmy that

Then she pulls her hand away from my man pole, and although I should be disappointed at this, I'm actually delighted because it gives me some respite from the possibility of prematurely ejaculating. She's pulled her hand away because she's enjoying what I'm doing so much and I start to congratulate myself, but at the same time ensure I continue whatever it is I'm doing that's obviously working. She then grabs onto my hand, stopping my rhythm, and looks into my eyes, kisses me and then looks behind her. At the far end of the park, there's a small area of bushes – assisted by the darkness and lack of lampposts surrounding the park, this small patch of grass is almost completely private from someone walking their dog, or other teenagers looking to cause mischief.

Without saying anything Tiny begins to pull me in the direction of the love nest, and I try to dispel any notion of vulgarity floating through my head of sharing a sexual experience with my girlfriend in the same location as many teenagers before – especially her older brother.

However, and in life there's always a fucking however…the thing about sex – especially teenage first time sex – is that until the deed is actually done, there's a multitude of things that can go wrong. I've already covered the physical insecurities of the male, but I haven't yet spoken about the emotional. The thing about being at the height of your sexual pleasure is that all of a sudden you begin to imagine you're invincible; the world is at your feet because your hips will be moving faster than normal, and you don't seem to have any limitations in action or in speech. You can't possibly comprehend how anything could go wrong, because the joining of two bodies is supposedly sacred; you think you're the man now and putting a condom on the end of it just seems like a daily habit: arrogance is already radiating from your body. But the reason sex isn't normally a planned thing, but a mood thing, is because it is of course as much about the emotional side as it is the physical. Sexual attractions aren't just physical; in fact, the way a person looks usually has little merit when it comes to desire.

So when Tiny was dragging me lasciviously towards the place we would first do it and she muttered something to me, I didn't for a second even consider the consequences when I answered, 'yer no a virgin'…because that's the truth: she's not. Someone has taken this away from her. There's no biological law that says penetration is not classed as penetration if it's against your will. Someone has already done to her what I was about to, and that's just reality. However, there's a time and place to remind someone of this, and I didn't half choose mine.

Fast forward thirty seconds and there's stillness. For once the two bodies in the love nest aren't actually moving about daringly; they're just sitting. Mr Solid has become Mr Floppy, and to contradict what I said before about classical music, I was actually referring to the screeching kind, where the record is broken. Someone has sucked all the lust out of the atmosphere and replaced it with sexual tension. Somehow I find myself sitting behind her, because she has turned away from me and is crying. There's a loose hair dangling from her shoulder and my instinct is to grab hold of it. On contact with her body, she lets out a little squeal, but doesn't move. She seems lost in her surroundings and I'm not exactly sure what to do next.

Jimmy this, Jimmy that

I'm wracking my brains trying to work out how to best help the situation, secretly praying Noggin or Specks might come back, having forgotten their jacket or left their house keys. But they won't, because that would be too easy an escape.

I decide – as the recently confirmed boyfriend – I have to reach above my scale of maturity and forget about intercourse. I have to think about the best way to repent for my actions and attempt to assuage the pain she's obviously suffering. I take her hand and kiss the back of her head, but still she doesn't move. So I attempt to throw her a lifeline – or is it myself I'm trying to save? – And open my mouth. 'Dae ye want tae talk aboot it?' – To which she merely looks at me and then looks away. This dismissive look makes me feel a pang of love for her. But do I even know what love means? To throw about the word love at such a young age, having experienced nothing of the world is unwise. How can I talk about love when we've been through nothing together?

But then something amazing happens…she turns and looks at me again, this time smiling and then kissing me on the cheek – almost saying she approves of my lame attempt at maturity; throwing me a modicum of approbation for trying to rescue the perilous situation, before muttering softly, 'lit's go and sit oan the swings.'

So that's what we do.

We watch a stray cat nibbling at something in a bucket, and enjoy the night enveloping us in with its crisp nippiness, and then she speaks. She tells me about that fateful night and how vividly it still rests within her. She tells me about the hate in the eyes of the perpetrator and how his strength was so overbearing. She tells me how he seemed in a hurry and scrambled her into darkness – ripping at her clothes like they had no value. How his breath was vile and he wore black motorcycle gloves. She couldn't fathom how someone could get turned on by such an act and didn't know whether to scream or cry. She alluded to him standing over her withering body once he had finished, and laughing at what he'd done. She was positive he hadn't come inside her, but the police told her to go to the clinic for testing anyway. When they said 'testing', they actually meant 'you've been raped, so will have to see a doctor and not just buy a pregnancy test from ASDA'. She said the doctor was embarrassed when she saw the bruising and became evasive – all the time pretending to be doing something else. I then ask her how she ended up on her own and she replies she can't really remember. She was at a party and thinks she could have taken something, or possibly been spiked. She didn't really agree with some of the people her friend Diane had invited, but wasn't going to comment on it because it wasn't her house. I say did she recognise the guy and manage to give the police a decent enough description, but she says no; she was too shocked and afraid, and he was wearing a skiing hat, pulled almost completely over his face. I then tell her I think she's dealt with the aftermath of it brilliantly and she bemusedly answers thank you. I then stupidly say it doesn't have any effect on how I feel about her, but she aggressively says that doesn't help. She wished it had never happened and was angry at me for reminding her of it at that exact moment, because that was what she had dreaded most.

Eventually she stops talking for a few seconds and looks into the sky; reminiscing about this unfortunate juncture in her life, and as I put my hand out towards her, she takes it and squeezes – more of a thank you for listening than anything else.

After a few minutes we begin to talk about school and move to sit on the bench outside the park – where she nervously sits on my knee. She tells me her hypothesis on life and how everything happens for a reason. She says she's disappointed in herself for crying because to linger in the past is dangerous and merely just an excuse for failure. She explains to me that to be different is a gift and not a burden, and her choice to occasionally wear extravagant clothes is her way of showing the world she isn't afraid to be an anomaly. She isn't willing to merely conform. It's during this diatribe that I recognise how much she has going for her, and how similar she is to Noggin; both bright but like everyone else, struggling with the immoralities and injustices of teenage life.

We didn't have sex tonight, but that would come; it's merely a formality. However, the fact that she's opened up to me is massive, and I recognise the significance of this emotional intimacy she's created between us. Her maturity is something I'm in awe of, and my summation of events this evening could accurately be written in two sentences:

It's my first taste of that complicated thing they call love.

At least the part when you hurt someone anyway.

18

Tiny and I are going on our first holiday. How great is the prospect of going on holiday with your other half; romantic walks by the sea, feeding each other strawberries and champagne, having sex in a different location, talking to other people about how you first met, going out for candlelit meals: all the stereotypical activities that perfectly fall into the category 'unequivocal holiday love'. Of course this isn't our holiday I'm referring to. I'm talking about some recently engaged couple who've chosen Berwick as the perfect destination for inspirational, passionate copulation, leading to the probability of a honeymoon baby. Tiny and I *are* going on holiday to Berwick, but we'll be joined by Noggin, Specks, and Joanna Hope also.

I might have sycophantically referred to Noggin's uncle as a legend for letting us into the pub atmosphere at such a young age, but this opportunity to use his caravan for a week is taking it to the next level. I don't have the pocket dictionary available to find the superlatives required to describe how I feel about the guy, so jokingly ask Noggin if I can send him a letter, exclaiming my undying love.

After laughing, Noggin nonchalantly says, 'he likes tae gee the young ones a chance, that's aw…'

'What else has he goat?' I reply, greedily.

'Gee a man an inch and he'll take a mile eh…'

'He doesnae need anymare inches,' Tiny mutters – and the holiday is off to a great start.

Specks, naturally playing piggy in the middle, has a very pale complexion on our travels, and I'm pretty positive it's about this rumour going around the school. Noggin had spoken to me about it last night, almost putting Specks on trial, asking me whether it had any authenticity in it, or whether it was just teenage angst getting out of control.

This is what had been doing the rounds at school:

Specks had been stalking a girl called Donna McLeish – pretty innocuous for our current age bracket – but apparently the stalking had begun to veer towards harassing, then closer to voyeuristic, then completely out of control. What started as just a simple 'hiya', apparently became an aggressive, 'Hey, A'm talkin tae you', and 'Stoap fuckin ignorin eez'. This probably doesn't seem much, but these desperate sentences were just the beginning. There used to be letters passed to her in geography, which materialised into a distant figure always waiting for her after gym class. A few flirtatious phone calls to her house turned into calls from an anonymous number and someone with their sleeve over their mouth asking if Donna is still a virgin. It went from watching her going into the female toilets, to following her into the female toilets. Then there were his threats of suicide, and messages on the walls saying that she had ruined his life and would be held accountable for the suffering of his family. At the age of fourteen, girls can usually just say, 'fuck off, leave me alone', but there's a lot of uncertainty surrounding Specks. People often say he's

Jimmy

unpredictable and not someone to get on the wrong side of. Of course, the problem with any obsession: it quickly gets out of control and eventually people can't deal with it any more. So only last week – after apparently receiving another anonymous call – Donna had phoned the police, and since then a whole novel's worth of stories were circulating the school, so you can imagine how delighted Specks was when the bell rang on Friday, liberating him for the summer holidays.

Of course when we arrive at the caravan, and Specks dumps his tattered looking sports bag on the floor, I can't help but notice a photograph of a girl trying to escape from one of the pouches, and my heart sinks. Noggin's right, I do always stick up for him, but someone has to… especially if he really is stupid enough to carry a photo around of the one person he most definitely shouldn't.

The interior of the caravan is ingenious, and how they manage to squeeze so many utilities, chairs, bedrooms and excess paraphernalia into such a small space always amazes me. From the outside it's no larger than the connecting part of a freight lorry. The chequered plastic upholstery is a bit disgusting, the curtains are a really ugly brown colour and you need binoculars to watch the T.V, but all in all, it's a rather decent holiday caravan and we're delighted.

The three bedroom thing is a huge bonus also, because it means Tiny and I can have our own room. I very much doubt anything excessively sensual will happen this week because the walls are paper thin, but that doesn't mean it hasn't happened already; only last Thursday we got down to it on the edge of a cliff, and a few days after that on

Cramond beach. It was magic, and there was no mention of….well it doesn't matter what there was no mention of, but the fact of the matter is, it wasn't mentioned.

Although the surrounding amenities are pretty convenient, most of the holiday will actually be spent inside, playing cards and drinking. The place is very family orientated, and we don't really fancy the under 10's recreational class.

Spending a day in Portobello with Joanna Hope is one thing, but a whole week is another; she might seem nice enough, but she's also one of those precocious acting teenagers who don't really drink much, certainly don't smoke, and sporadically nip out to the shop returning with a packet of dried mango. Somehow her anomalous status suits her, though, and nobody seems to mind when she goes outside in the morning and performs a rigorous Yoga routine. Actually it looks really beneficial, but there's no way any of us are going to join in. Tiny and Joanna get on fine, but their cordiality towards each other in the early days is out of respect, not out of chemistry, and we often whisper about this in the night. Not that she's disruptive in any way, but maybe she's just a bit too nice and we aren't used to such a heightened sensitivity or severe approach to things. An example is when we're playing cards and she mentions going to church. Sensing disapproval, she quickly says before moving to Edinburgh her parents had forced her to attend on Sundays, and that it's just something everybody should try at least once.

I'm almost positive she's about to embark on some diatribe about how the only path to God is through Jesus Christ, when Specks interrupts, saying, 'church? Cunt, bibles and that shit. No fur me likes. Mind that time we went wae Jimmy,' – but I interrupt and quickly change the subject.

She definitely shows a maturity way beyond her years though; talking to the family next door, cleaning the toilet, and even making meals with vegetables. I mean, seriously, who makes meals with vegetables on holiday? She speaks about going to University to study English literature, travelling to Australia, and how important she thinks voluntary work is for the community.

No wonder Noggin likes her so much. Her frequent patronising reaction to the ridiculous comments rolling off Specks' drunken tongue kept me going throughout, and there's several memorable occasions; such as, when Specks says, 'A dinnae git the whole continent hing,' and Joanna says, 'what is there not to get?' – Producing this response from him: 'well furgiv me fur bein the intellectual among us, but how kin Africa be classed as a continent if every cunt is fuckin starvin?'

This is met with silence and a look of amazement/ serious concern at his seemingly incomprehensible geographical views.

Another favourite is when Joanna asks him what he wants to do with his life and he says, 'probly be a fuckin plumber eh. How hard kin it be tae fix windaes?'

I suppose if we weren't used to his level of IQ; we'd probably give him patronising glances as well. To be fair to her though, she does always make an effort with him, which is more than I can say for Noggin. Maybe it's a religious thing, a humanitarian act, where she thinks she can teach him the ways of the world and guide him.

My personal favourite of the week is when Joanna is bored of playing card games and asks if we want to hear her dramatic reading for Drama class. This is my favourite moment because not only does Noggin look petrified at the prospect of his girlfriend doing a dramatic reading, but Specks adds, 'aye, goan then, but it better no be that fuckin Statespeare.'

The reading doesn't go ahead, and for once, Noggin looks at Specks favourably. To be fair, he was only two consonants out.

As much as I enjoy most elements of the week, I look forward to bedtime every night the most; occasionally faking tiredness just so I could close the door behind us and get under the covers. It isn't about the physical with Tiny – although that is always a bonus – it's about the emotional. We have a real emotional connection. Joanna Hope might be an intellectual compared to Tiny, but my girlfriend has a virility that Joanna doesn't have; a dignity, inner fortification and confidence. She is fascinated by philosophy, psychology and metaphysics. I can listen to her for hours rambling on and on about her passions in life; about the intricacies of the human mind. She's an avid follower of astrology and has a small tattoo of the Aries constellation on her hip. There's still a fair amount of foreplay and muffled moaning, but this is always intertwined with her talking about Noggin and his choice of girls, Specks and his impossible chances for the future, and me and my constant need to be the inconspicuous one. I suppose she's right about that; I don't ever want to stand out; I always try and avoid confrontation if necessary, and up until now haven't really pushed myself. She says

I have potential, but all the time I'm thinking 'it's you that's got potential. You that's never content; you that's desperate to evolve'.

A picture and a single sentence will reside inside me long after the holiday finishes; of Tiny and Joanna going for a walk together and then overhearing Joanna saying to Noggin, 'you never told me your sister was smart. She's got a lot to say about the world.'

I guess it filled me with pride, because whether I liked to admit it or not, we did all see Joanna as intellectually and emotionally superior. The dynamics with her and Noggin are very interesting throughout; the intelligent one in our group of boys suddenly being challenged. I revered Joanna for bringing Noggin down a notch, because he occasionally won arguments with words we didn't understand, or logics we couldn't be certain of, but his inner dictionary seems to have been left in Edinburgh on this occasion. It's also important to mention that she's a really affirming person, and as the week goes on I can see why Noggin is so taken with her. Intellectual stimulation is hard to come by, and for the moment, both Noggin and I have landed on our feet.

Of course we aren't always confined to the plastic upholstery and the very small toilet; we hang about the amusements a fair amount – Joanna reads her book, leaving Noggin perpetually fractious – and Tiny and I go on the motorbike simulator, the dancing machine, and even pretend to be a married couple, going to the bar and ordering a cappuccino and a latte. We never drink them; we're just practicing for future holidays. There's also an amazing chippy, which sells the most delectable haddock.

It makes me think twice about the actual quality of the supper at our local. It's quite a pricey wee joint, though, so most of the time we stick to microwave meals or forcing Joanna's vegetable risotto down our throats. I'm pretty sure this sudden intake of vegetables has an adverse effect on my constitution because something pretty drastic happens every time I go to the toilet.

There's quite a tense moment in our third day, when a woman is running about looking for her lost son and all the employees of the holiday park are suddenly placed on high alert, because previously a six year old had drowned in the sea – meaning the entire place had to be shut down and under investigation for longer than was comfortable. She eventually finds him hiding under a caravan. It appears he'd taken the family's game of hide and seek to the next level.

As the early holiday awkwardness disappears, and we grow collectively as a group, everything seems to fit into place and habitual routines are always treated with normality – apart from the vegetables, which I don't think are normal at all and probably never will. It's very amusing when we go to the counter in the **Spar** with three cans of coke, one can of Fanta, four mars bars and a courgette.

On the final day Joanna and Tiny go into Berwick city centre. We all think this very grown up of them and once again, I gleam with pride when they announce that Tiny has certain things she wants to discuss about her future. They need some girl on girl time. My natural pessimistic instinct would be to think it's to discuss whether I'm good enough for her or not, but after the chat we had last night, I'm pretty confident it isn't. Since their first walk, Joanna has taken a serious liking to Tiny; I even noticed a separate bookmark in *Pride and Prejudice* – so much for the cider drinking and playing cards.

Whilst they're out – ordering green tea and pretending to be older than they actually are – the three of us enjoy a moment reminiscent of the immediate post-Jimmy days. I think about everything involved in the past few months at school; old friendships and new, girls and girlfriends, Jimmy and not Jimmy, and how without noticing we just evolve. Evolution happens in such infinitesimal steps that we don't notice any significant difference from day to day. Maturity is usually augmented by experience and we have certainly shared a lot of that over the last year or so. Then there's a natural split – as though we yearn to be alone. I'm desperate for a burger, Noggin goes for a beer shit and Specks just sits there, watching the particles in the air, the dust mites looking to settle. There's stillness inside the caravan. The only sound the churning of the microwave motor and the distant laughter of a child on the beach. Noggin has the door closed and I have my back to Specks. All of a sudden it feels like we aren't an entity anymore; like we don't actually know how to spend a significant amount of time together. Our closeness has been overruled by this new dynamic we find ourselves in and I think about how life moves along, from one juncture to another – whether we like it or not. I can feel Specks behind me thinking the same thing, and Noggin sitting on the toilet ruminating. I can picture Joanna and Tiny sitting together, probably laughing amongst themselves about the habits of the male, the complexities of their intimate relationships and how strange it is to be here at this exact moment. I think about the relevance of the word moment and that this is all we ever have: the moment, and yet we think about anything but.

Then I notice movement outside, and decide to open the curtain slightly and investigate. A police officer is talking to a woman in the opposite caravan and I begin to wonder if something is wrong, when he turns and looks at me. For a moment I freeze. My previous moment of profundity has evaporated, and now I'm filling up with something like fear. The lady in the opposite caravan is pointing at me – a stern finger, fraught with accusation. And then I turn my attention away from the window and say, 'Noggin'…but nothing else. I feel the change in gravity as Specks rises from his seat and a fear from the past returns to me. Where everything I ever stood for felt on the line and my very existence was questioned.

The microwave pings at exactly the same time as the door rattles and for a moment I hope its Tiny and Joanna, and this policeman isn't coming to look for us. But then it strikes me…something has undoubtedly happened to one of the girls and this police officer is here to tell us the bad news. This holiday is going to end with a tragedy and unless I scream out, 'you've goat the wrong fuckin caravan', this isn't going to go away. I want to shout out something meaningful, but the door has rattled again. I look at Noggin, who's looking at me and attempting to quickly buckle up his belt. I wonder how we can justify an accident to one of the girls, and if we will be held accountable. I think if it's Tiny, Noggin will have to take the blame because he's the older brother; I think if it's Joanna, Noggin will also feel terrible. I can feel myself beginning to panic and I suddenly stop. It might be nothing;

Jimmy

he might just be enquiring about something or wanting to ask questions about some incident we haven't heard about…but then why the accusatory finger from the woman opposite? Why was there no empathy or sympathy in that point, and why do I suddenly feel like I'm drowning? Why the fuck is he tapping for a third time and still nobody has answered? It's because it has to be me. Whatever and however tragic the information standing behind that door is, it has to me that faces it; it just has to be.

Slowly I open the door and don't even look for a face filled with empathy, because I find myself shouting, 'please tell eez nout's happened tae Jane!'

But then I pause, and then smile, because Noggin is laughing at me and I know why he is. He's laughing at the significance of me calling his sister by her Christian name and how odd it sounds; how mature it sounds, and how wrong also. She's said to me repeatedly throughout the holiday that Tiny isn't for her anymore and can I please call her Jane – especially in front of Joanna.

But this thought all but evaporates when the police officer steps into the caravan, unannounced. There isn't any mention of 'there's been an accident', or 'I'm sorry for your loss…', or 'are you the brother or the boyfriend of…'

There isn't even an introduction or a 'how are you today sir'. There's just the slow movement of his feet, and then he's inside, closing the door behind him.

And then it dawns on me…and I smile…more a smile of relief than anything else. As the officer begins moving from room to room, I realise he isn't here to tell us about an accident in our group. He's here to tell us of a felony. As he moves in and out the first two rooms, and approaches the third, it strikes me right between the eyes: he's here for Specks. I hadn't even thought about it because my judgement had been clouded by fear of anything happening to the two girls, and I laugh to myself for not recognising this straight away.

We follow the police officer through to the third bedroom and watch in amazement as object after object is lifted from the bag. Specks must have been stealing something every time he went into the shop and the normally trustworthy Berwickshire counter assistant had eventually got suspicious about the bulge in his pocket. The police officer then turns to me and says, 'is this your bag?'

But I don't actually have time to answer, because there's movement behind us and Specks is trying to escape out the front door of the caravan. However, unfortunately for him, he hasn't bargained on the fact that another officer is lurking outside.

The tall, lanky policeman then looks at us, and we can both tell he has a huge amount to say, because he hesitates and then hesitates again. The only thing that saves us from uncomfortable questioning is a tap at the door, and within a matter of seconds he's disappeared – marching Specks to the local police station.

Is it just the stealing? Or is it his voyeurism also? Has Donna Mcleish pressed charges? Or is it to do with his dad? Is the officer carrying evidence relating to his disappearance?

All this goes through my head as I sit down on the wooden floor, resting my back against the wall. I can still see evidence of his latest felony lying on the bed. Not just the stuff from the shop – which I imagine is mostly things for his mum – but the photograph of Donna McLeish… the girl that was never his. This image perfectly sums up his life: chasing affirmation in all the wrong places, all the wrong ways.

A few minutes go by, and as Noggin puts his hand on my shoulder and says, 'C'moan mate, lit's go and find them two,' I want to shout at him, and then throw him against the wall: 'A dinnae want yer fuckin hand. Look at that bed: it's no me that needs it.'

But of course I don't, because I guess it's just how things are in the world; some people get the hand on their shoulder, others don't.

As Noggin helps me to my feet, I think about how for some people it just isn't meant to be easy, and then begin to go over the immorality of the conversation we had the night before. He told me that Joanna had asked him if he fancied spending the rest of the summer in her uncle's cottage and that she would really like it if Tiny and I could come also. The thing that struck me most about this conversation was that at no point did he say anything about an invitation for Specks.

that

19

I did not enjoy Art class. This had nothing to do with a lack of aesthetic creativity. In fact, if truth be told, I secretly enjoyed pretending to be Van Gogh. The reason we didn't like Art class was because Mr Hallegon was a complete wanker. To use words like patronising and condescending would possibly be a little generous of me, so I'll just say this; he obviously had ambitions out-with the current curriculum, and rumour had it he begrudged having to teach us delinquents – as he often unceremoniously referred to us – and only actually worked here because framing costs were so expensive. Somebody really should have reported him to the headmaster. However, in retrospect, I can see he was just a frustrated artist, and why would anybody want to teach us lot anyway?

Only a very small proportion of the class actually cared about passing Art, so as a form of rebellion we intentionally went out of our way to wind him up. This would involve the painting of a courgette with two little round bumps at the bottom; or an inaccurate anatomical recreation of the vagina, which when scrutinised we would claim was the opening of a flower for pollination.

On this particular day, Hallegon is languidly attempting to teach us something about the dexterity of Italian fresco painters, when Darren Ingles turns to me and says, 'what the fuck does dexterity mean?'

'Who cares,' I respond.

Noggin is sitting on the other side of the class, paying attention and taking notes. I accepted a long time ago he was 'a wanky studier' – hence why he rarely sits beside me. But he's also a friend, so I try not to pass judgement as often as I'd like to. But paying attention in Art class is taking it to another level, and this just can't be accepted.

So combining my anger towards Noggin's studious nature with my hatred for Hallegon, I decide to create something that will potentially upset proceedings.

Pertinent to the name of the class we currently sit in, I've taken two lollipop sticks and glued them together with an elastic band: thus creating the very brilliant, but obviously disposable, slingshot. My name might never end up in the history books like Alexander Graham Bell, or Hallegon's idol Rembrandt, but for this particular plan, my invention is highly expedient.

Perfectly equipped with Blu-Tack – which Ingles is rolling into little balls for me – I'm now ready to attack.

'Are ma baws ready fur use?' I mutter.

He smiles and says loudly, 'yer baws are prepared and very round sir.'

This evokes a look of disgust from Hallegon, who merely shakes his head, before going back to talking shite.

Ingles sniggers and hands me the balls. I insert the ammunition into the weapon of not-so-mass-destruction and take aim, my eyes squinting slightly in order to get the perfect angle – like looking through a pair of binoculars. I pull back the elastic band…stretching it further and further, hoping to obtain complete control over gravity and the consistency of levitation, when suddenly I halt, because Ingles has just spoken to me again: said something meaningful...I think.

'What wis that?' I mutter with gritted teeth.

'Are ye gawn tae the fight the night?'

'What fight?'

'Remember Jimmy Stokes that goat expelled last year?'

Alarm bells ringing. Church bells ringing. Life bells ringing.

'Did ye just say Jimmy Stokes?'

On hearing the name Noggin turns his head towards me, and then looks away. Does he know about this?

'Aye...him that sold every cunt the fags.'

'Who's he fighting?'

'Some top boy fi Wester Hailes.'

Again, I glance over at Noggin. He looks at me and I can see it in his face: he knows about it; he definitely knows about it.

I can't tell if he approves of this fight and wants to witness it, or whether that fleeting glance he gave me says 'don't even fucking think about it'.

But why wouldn't we want to see Jimmy fight? We can always stand at the back.

I'm trying to telepathically put these questions to Noggin, but a sudden dismissive head shaking warns me off.

I, for one, would love to see Jimmy being punched about; but what of Noggin? Will he be annoyed if I suggest we attend? Is that not what people do? Watch fights. With absolute impunity, the ancient Romans used to watch people being barbarically slaughtered in the Colloseum, so why shouldn't we enjoy the spectacle of Jimmy Stokes fighting someone who already holds the title 'Top Boy'? Jimmy might get annihilated. How could we possibly miss that?

Someone is passing me a folded piece of paper. I suspect it's from Noggin, and when I open it my suspicions are confirmed because all that's written on it is, *We'll talk aboot it after class.*

I scrunch up the piece of paper and look at Noggin, who nods his head as if to say 'Ok…' and then turns back to paying attention.

All this has taken place in the first few minutes of the period, so I've got a bit of time to wait before we can discuss it. I don't even feel like utilising my brilliant invention anymore. I just want to sit there…and think.

It's interesting, because twenty years later Kevin would randomly ask me if I remembered the first time I met Jimmy, and the truth is I can't. He just merged into our lives, effortlessly, like the sun rising over the distant sea. The funny thing is, after that night at Peebo's flat; he just as effortlessly merged himself out of our lives.

20

'What time's it at?'

'Seven.'

'Where?'

'The field – just up fi the doactors.'

A teacher walks past us, stops, but chooses to move on instead of enquire. A bird swoops and squawks in our direction – sending a signal out to his friend's school is over for the day and they can search for the remnants of lunch with impunity. The janitor crosses the forecourt, dressed in all blue. Specks is also crossing the forecourt, just behind the janitor, smiling and holding a VHS. Of course: the 'after school dodgy movies dealing club'. A group of individuals who pretend to be doing something illegal, when actually there's no felony involved in swapping videos amongst friends. Of course, it depends on the content of the videos.

On approaching he shouts, 'are youse gawn?'

Obviously we both know what he's referring to, but Noggin still says, 'where?'

'The fuckin fight! Wee fuckin Pete wis just tellin eez aboot what happened. Apparently Jimmy wis up Wester Hailes last weekend smashin a boys windae. The cunt just happened tae be one eh the top boys. Word goat spread aboot and a paggar is gonnae take place the night. I wonder if Jimmy's gonnae pay fur the cunts windae. *No likely.*'

He stands in anticipation, waiting for our response, but this spiel has rendered us speechless.

Eventually I say, 'are you gawn?'

'Obviously. Every cunts gawn.'

Does he understand this is the same Jimmy Stokes who left him for dead? Maybe this is an indication of his emotional intelligence that he seems more taken in by the significance of the event than the significance of the protagonist.

'A couple eh the boys are headin up tae try and git bevvy before it. Ye fancy it?'

'Na,' is all I say.

'Fuck ye then,' he says, and smiles. 'Nogs?'

'You go fur it, mate.'

This last sentence was said with gritted teeth, because Noggin absolutely hated it when someone called him Nogs. It's not only an indication of being too comfortable, it's also an insult to his nickname. Giving a nickname to a nickname is not desirable.

'You cunts awright?'

'Aye, mate,' Noggin says. 'Just a bit eh a surprise…'

A moment of silence ensues, making me feel slightly irritated. Specks lingers, looking over his shoulder – a movement we've become too familiar with. We choose not to ask, and eventually he follows as we move towards the school gate.

Since Specks joined the after-school VHS club, Noggin and I have enjoyed some really decent chats on the way home, so we're secretly disappointed he's chosen to join us.

Yesterday he told me about his cousin in America who opened his own window cleaning business and now makes a fortune. Apparently he started tapping on people's doors and offering to wash their windows for $5. Thinking about how often my mum complains about the windows, I can see how this would be a profitable market. Now he doesn't wash any windows. Just sits in his office and orders subordinates about.

21

The number 37 bus ascends the incline, collecting a variety of passengers on the way, before turning left and picking up speed along the main road; a man in his late 60s is walking his dog, smoking a cigar and intermittently spitting; an overweight woman is pulling a personal shopper, wearing a hand-me-down overcoat and shouting at someone on her mobile phone; a motorbike is slowing down at the traffic lights, the driver lifting up his visor.

These people might all have their own agendas, their differing destinations, and their personal errands to run. However, there is one thing they all have in common: at one point they've all glanced over at the field, wondered what is to occur.

Nothing untoward has actually taken place on this stretch of grass yet, but the signs are undoubtedly ominous. There's a group of about sixty males gathered, and I very much doubt their intention is to pick up discarded dog shit. What makes this a forbidding sight is not necessarily the amount of people gathered, but the type: skinheads, tattoos, stone island jackets, bottles of vodka, caps, and scars: all stereotypical thugs.

You can't see it, but I wonder how many weapons are hidden underneath the jackets and anyone intending

that

to cross the field and go to the shops will definitely think twice.

In fact, they won't think twice, they'll think once. That thought will be to avoid this area altogether…at least until events unfold.

A slightly older guy seems to be making the rounds, and obviously fancies himself as the one running proceedings. Seems to think there's not one square foot of this field out with his jurisdiction and I begin to wonder if another fight might be on the cards.

I get closer and, believe it or not, he seems to be preaching some sort of code of conduct. He's imperiously suggesting the following; that there's no need for anything other than a fair square-go between Jimmy and TAGS. If either guy says it's enough, it's enough. The temerity of this guy is unbelievable, but nobody seems to be taking him seriously. Maybe this is something to do with his eyeballs – which are bulbous – giving off the air of someone high. Based on how much he's talking, I would imagine he's been taking speed.

In all honesty, I'm praying Noggin wants to leave before the fight even begins, because what are we doing here anyway?

Everyone just seems to be waiting around – which only accentuates the paranoia I'm currently dealing with – when I overhear a voice saying it's because TAGS hasn't arrived yet. Obviously one of those people who enjoys turning up late for his own party. Also, the fact that he won't come on his own means the sixty will rise to about seventy. The fact the field is just along from a police station doesn't bode well either. Mind you, they might intentionally

Jimmy this, Jimmy that

ignore a provocation like this. I certainly would. Also, nothing has actually happened yet, so there's no need to intervene. Or maybe he's not coming. Maybe he's afraid of Jimmy. There's a big difference between threatening someone and actually following through. Maybe this is why Jimmy looks so happy, because he didn't bottle it. He's here: ready to rumble. But where's TAGS? Surely he's got a reputation to sustain also?

In an attempt to assuage the butterflies in my stomach, I circumnavigate my surroundings. Curtains are being pulled back and more people than is natural are having cigarettes out their windows. As my head rotates nearly 180 degrees – past the sleeping police station and over the playground of the secondary School opposite – I catch a glimpse of an approaching crowd. Even from afar, the smoking, drinking, and swaggering, leaves me with no doubt that one of them must be Jimmy's opponent. For some reason my instinct is to look at Jimmy. Do I feel slightly protective of him? Or was this glance just me trying to ascertain whether his countenance would change now that he's aware the fight won't be cancelled after all. As I'm looking over, Peebo pats him on the back and says something encouraging into his ear.

Within a matter of minutes, the final group arrive and shake a few hands, throw in a few high fives and produce a few bottles of alcohol. There are comments about 'it no being a barbecue', and 'did ye forget tae set yer alarm', but nothing more threatening than that.

A few of them glance over at Jimmy– who is unmoved by their appearance on the field. They all seem to want a piece of him.

that

As the minutes pass by, apart from the obvious hateful energy shooting back and forward between Jimmy and his assailant, there isn't really anything to report. A lot of people have their hands in their pockets, or are smoking cigarettes. The calm before the storm?

'What yins TAGS?' I say to Noggin.

'The fuckin massive guy at the back.'

'Wi the timberlands?'

'Aye.'

'Jimmy's fightin him?'

'Aye…Jimmy's fightin him.'

'Fuckin ell.'

After a breath, we both laugh, but not the sort of laugh that would come after a perfectly executed anecdote. We laugh because surely Jimmy is out of his league here? Surely it's just all for show and he'll bottle it at the last minute? This guy looks like he's done time, and has the tattoos and biceps to show for it.

But this is what Jimmy really wants. What he thrives on: a whole audience of his people; watching him, revering him. This isn't a collection of ordinary citizens who Jimmy normally intimidates, bullies and terrorizes with impunity. This is a group of people on his level. Or what he thinks is his level. This is the hierarchy, the fucking top end of the scale. Even if he loses this fight it will still change his reputation forever. Even if the guy breaks his jaw, Jimmy will still be a winner. He'll still be known as someone who doesn't fear anyone. Our laugh was a bemused one, because we knew Jimmy wouldn't bottle it. We knew this fight would go ahead.

It might have taken a few minutes to register, but once it did, there was one obvious thing we couldn't hide away from: this wasn't just a fight between Jimmy and some guy from a different area; this was gangster shit, and although he arrived with a few of the other guys from school and wasn't actually standing beside us, looking over at Specks, I could tell that just like Noggin and I, he was fucking bricking it.

22

If you were lucky enough to be flying over the field in a helicopter, you would notice two symmetrical lines of people, with one person from each of these lines standing forward a metre or two, facing one other. This picture of organised warfare would be finished off with two people lingering behind the lines, looking for any potential movement from the police station. The greatest part of this image would be its biblical reference, because even from a few hundred yards in the sky, you'd still be able to make out one of these guys in the middle was David, and the other undoubtedly Goliath.

Me? I'm intermittently glancing from Jimmy to the police station, Jimmy to the police station, because although I haven't committed any crime, if it does get hairy and we have to scatter, the police will take anyone they can.

Imagine the irony of me spending the night in the cells at the expense of Jimmy Stokes.

So who was going to take the crown? In one corner you've got TAGS: skinhead; 19 years of age; Stone Island jacket; Tattoos on his knuckles and arms; only smokes the hard stuff; part of the most feared family in the city: the Bennetts; real name – Deek Bennett. Got into his first fight at ten, when a boy in primary school called his mum a fat cow, so TAGS stapled his ear to a table and broke all his fingers with a hammer. Thinks stealing is a dirty habit and doesn't condone it in his friends; has subordinates selling drugs for him, whilst he spends the profit on fancy clothes for his girlfriend. To all intents and purposes, the type of guy who deserves the tag *Godfather.*

Then in the other corner you've got Jimmy Stokes; only got a skinhead because his mate Peebo has one; 15 years of age; Stone Island Jacket? Only if stolen from someone's washing line. Tattoos? Not even old enough to walk through the door of a tattoo shop. Smokes anything he can get his hands on; not part of any feared family: an only child. In fact, when he was born, his mum probably said 'fuck me, this yin cannae have a brother or sister'. Probably got into his first fight when he was born and didn't like the look of the doctor. Loves stealing and obviously condones it among his peers; attempted to sell drugs on numerous occasions, but ran out of people who could trust him; a bully and a womanizer; a thief and a morally corrupt maniac.

Jimmy's an opportunist: in the boxing world they call it a journeyman; grab a quick dollar for stepping into the ring. So what's his advantage then, if he actually has one? Well, he knows from reputation TAGS is a bear knuckle man, so the snivelling little deceitful bastard has probably got a knife in his pocket, because he knows he's got more chance winning a fair fight against a buffalo. So like most situations in his poor excuse for a life, Jimmy has probably come prepared to cheat.

23

The thing about predictability is that it sets an emotional precedent: a certain amount of expectation. If the way someone acts in a certain situation never falters, we don't expect anything different from them: ever. I would never have labelled Jimmy as predictable – because in our precarious involvement with him every day felt different and his spontaneity for barbarity was somewhat frightening – but when it came to fighting or any form of physical confrontation, Jimmy was predictable as ever; he'd act all innocent and then pull out a knife. But what if this predictability had run its course? What if the only reason for this predictability was because a pattern was necessary to accentuate the greatness of the moment when breaking this pattern? What if it had been subterfuge all along? What if despite everything; this choice of moment was predestined, written in the stars. What if it was just meant to be?

So here we are, waiting for the rumble to get started; the big fight of the fucking century: faggot balls Jimmy versus TAGS. Us three praying he gets annihilated for a childhood full of bullying, stealing and just plain being a dick, when suddenly everything goes silent and only two sounds can be heard: one; the seagulls, hoping this

Jimmy this, Jimmy that

large group of people will leave some food behind: and two; the sound of Jimmy zipping open his jacket. I should have known: we all should have known. Of course, the big occasion: the Piece-de-resistance.

Jimmy Stokes is holding a gun.

24

So what would you know, Jimmy Stokes was saving it for the big audience. The funny thing was: what kind of reaction did he expect to get from about seventy teenagers; a standing ovation for owning a gun; a round of applause for carrying something that could put him away for years; a pat on the back? What he really yearned for was everyone to get down on their knees, raise their hands and say 'Heil Hitler!' Did this happen though? No, absolutely fucking not. Aside from the fact the majority of the population laughed when he pulled it out, the only person they could see getting shot was TAGS, because after all, he was the one Jimmy had beef with. If it had been me, and someone had just pulled out a gun and waved it in my direction, I'd be on my knees reciting passages from the bible. So this is obviously what TAGS did, right? Wrong, he turned around and said to somebody, 'kin ye believe this fuckin guy?' – Thus producing a melodious second round of laughter from both sides of Jimmy Stokes. As you can imagine, Hitler was furious. He started waving the gun about like James Bond, but surprisingly, still nobody seemed to care, except Noggin and I obviously, although in a strange kind of way we were sort of intrigued; transfixed almost. We should have been more afraid, but weren't; it was as though this didn't suit Jimmy, and somehow his preconceived idea that the crowd would be terrified was disappearing with every laugh, and Jimmy couldn't even find any words to supplement his weapon: he resorted to just moving about theatrically.

There seems to be a rising air of mockery towards Jimmy, and it begins to feel like we're attending a pantomime. But then he does speak…to himself – which is so strange and uncharacteristic of him that I momentarily freeze. He seems to be questioning himself; not his motives, but whether he should unleash hell or not. He's obviously lost his audience, and wonders how best to get it back. He looks like the last surviving barbarian, standing alone in the Coliseum, looking around and hoping for approval from the emperor that he can remain alive, even though his duty as a slave was to die.

'Shoot me then ya daft wee cunt,' TAGS bemusedly says, much to the amusement of one guy in particular, who shouts, 'A told ye he wis a fuckin nutcase.'

'Is that a tattie gun?' TAGS mutters.

Irate at this latest disrespectful comment, Jimmy attempts to up the tempo, by producing two bullets from his pocket and saying, 'd'ye hink A'l no shoot ye ya cunt?'

TAGS laughs and retorts, 'what kind eh gangster walks aboot wi an unloaded gun?'

Jimmy is momentarily paralysed, as though he's played a King – imagining it to be unbeatable – only to witness TAGS throwing an ACE on the table. Again he seems to be thinking. Like most things in life, this apparent Square-go is not going to plan, and Jimmy must be regretting not bringing his knife instead. Jimmy then starts looking around, and as his eyes dart over several faces, I begin to wonder if he's looking for a scapegoat. I'm starting to wonder if his very limited neurons have mustered together an idea that if he shoots somebody weak, this might frighten TAGS; show him he's got the minerals. Jimmy then puts the bullets into the gun and although it probably should have materialised a lot earlier, this is the first occasion in the evening I can actually remember feeling genuine fear. It's probably because of trust: Jimmy can't be trusted with a loaded gun. I think we all know the scapegoat his eyes will land on. After all, a bully picks on people that won't retaliate; people who will revere you no matter what. People like Specks. After everything that happened in Peebo's flat, is Jimmy finally going to finish him off? He's bullied him so often in the past that Specks is obviously a reliable source. From the corner of my eye I can see Specks standing there, potentially thinking the same thing. Or is he hoping for it? Jimmy turns fully around and is looking through the line of people: one by one. It's almost like a line of Jews waiting to be handpicked for the gas chamber, and he has the eyes of a sergeant with strict orders. His eyes rest on me, and I look at him. I say to him without actually opening my mouth, 'dinnae even fuckin hink aboot it. If ma life is tae end the day, it certainly winnae be as your scapegoat'.

He quickly gets the picture and moves on to Noggin. Another guy he used to torment – not physically but certainly emotionally. You can tell he's thinking; wondering if this will go his way, because two bouts of ignominy is too much to cope with and TAGS will only take him seriously if someone else shows fear. I look at Noggin.

His eyes are like marble; smooth but unmoveable. He's telepathically saying exactly the same thing to Jimmy. In fact, from what I can see, it's worse. He's beseeching him to try it. He's intellectually transferring into Jimmy's head the kind of jail sentence he can expect from shooting someone, and taking this on board, Jimmy moves away. This whole demonic eye-darting thing has almost been pointless, because although Jimmy's choice of weapon turned out to be unpredictable, his choice of scapegoat won't be. It might have been a fair amount of time since Peebo's flat and no doubt there have been many hapless individuals bullied since then, but there's only really one candidate on this field: the boy who put up with his torment for months. The teenager who when presented with the chance – almost guaranteed impunity let's not forget– to physically damage him with his slingshot, had failed to take the bull by the horns; instead passing the opportunity for revenge onto someone else. But was Jimmy really going to shoot him? Was Jimmy really going to shoot anyone? Was it all just an act, and now that he's not getting the reaction he thought he would, he's panicking? Whatever the need for a scapegoat at this particular juncture might be, surely there are other candidates, because Specks did at one point come under the category 'friend', and although the nature of this word would definitely come under scrutiny, Jimmy surely still owes him for his time with this title. He surely still owes him some form of apology for Peebo's flat?

His eyes are locked on Specks, and unlike Noggin and I, he looks away. He submitted when he should have prevailed. He should have said to him, 'are ye fuckin jokin mate? Are ye seriously considerin humiliatin eez again? Wis the spatter eh blood on Peebo's flare no enough punishment fur one lifetime?'

But he doesn't, because he doesn't have the valour. He doesn't have the courage to recognise that bullies are actually weak. They only pick on people who will serve a purpose. They curl into little balls when challenged, and this is exactly what's happened to Jimmy; TAGS has laughed in his face and Jimmy is looking for an escape route. He's not going to shoot Specks, he just temporarily needs him for personal elevation in the social ladder.

'Specks...c'mere ye wee prick.'

Jimmy Stokes is definitely starting to wilt under pressure.

What do bullies do when things don't go their way? They lash out at every angle. However, what does a bully do in the face of adversity when his options are limited? He hesitates and becomes incomprehensible, because the world around him starts to recognise his limitations and actually all that is required to defeat him is to stand firm – If you have the bottle. But does Specks realise this?

'Did ye no hear what A said, ye wee cunt?'

Was that a shiver in Jimmy's voice?

And then it happens: Specks responds; the type of response that will be savoured forever. Not talked about, but remembered; implanted into the back of our heads and never dislodged; looked back upon with a smile of remembrance but a sour taste of sorrow.

'Fuck you, Jimmy,' Specks mutters.

'What the fuck did ye jist say?'

'He said, fuck you.'

Jimmy this, Jimmy that

Jimmy turns and TAGS has taken a step closer to him. This unnerves Jimmy. I'm struggling to keep up with proceedings, because Noggin is tugging at my sleeve and telling me to look to my left. I do so, and Specks is crying. From fear or happiness I'll never know, but then suddenly he turns and leaves. He's obviously making a run for it and hoping nobody knows he was reduced to tears by this decision. It's amazing how emotions work. It's possible he feels in this great time of need, he's let Jimmy down – even though it could have meant personal sacrifice. This is the moment he could have finally gained the bastard's respect and he turned his back on him. Hung him out to dry. The fact that Specks managed to explore his emotions in this way was amazing, but then again, maybe they overpowered him; maybe they refused to stay intact. Maybe Specks thought this was his destiny and the elevator to the afterlife was waiting for him to board, only for him to refuse to step on.

'Is it true ye rape wee lassies in the graveyard, Jimmy?'

Noggin looks at me, his eyes suddenly bulging. Surely not? He's asking me. *Surely fucking not?* But my countenance hasn't changed, because I've already thought about the possibility of it, the probability of it.

25

So these two adults have jumped out a taxi; fat, ugly, and quite frankly superfluous. When it comes to attire and general aura, they obviously have rules of their own; definitely not police, that's for sure. My first inclination is to ask them a question: why would you jump out a taxi into a crowd of adrenaline pumping youths, most of them not even conquered puberty yet? What do you think this is: a fucking football match?

Even the more confident people in the group are looking around them, trying to ascertain some sort of confirmation that these two guys aren't a threat, aren't a contingency, or some sort of barbaric surprise. Whoever they are, and whatever they want, they're outsiders and this venue has already surpassed its maximum capacity.

Some of the older guys are muttering to each other, 'who are these cunts?' and, 'does any cunt ken who these two bams are?' But nobody seems to answer in the affirmative.

The funniest part about it is the two rotund drunkards don't seem to appreciate what it is they've walked into, and are trying to get answers out of anyone and everyone. One of them is harping on about being from the West Lothian, and in his inebriated state he seems to be pushing

Jimmy this, Jimmy that

and shoving about, regurgitating some story about his brother Tony and how many years he spent in the army.

The evening has become about as predictable as the Scottish weather. The military lines of war have begun to disperse and gangs from opposing sides are beginning to mingle, even banter. Guys that only a matter of minutes ago were threatening each other are talking about trivialities like football and boxing, and I'm not entirely sure if these two guys recognise the effect they've had on proceedings. To be fair, quite a few of the group go to the same school, or have relations in the same area, so a lull in proceedings doesn't really faze them, but gives them a chance to catch up with exemption from being questioned. We came to see Jimmy's blood spill and all were getting is opinions on last night's football match.

Come to think of it, where *is* Jimmy?

I look a few yards to my right and he's standing talking to TAGS. They seem to be laughing about Jimmy's gun and he's showing it off. I almost can't believe what I'm seeing. What does this mean? Is Jimmy's fight no longer in the pipeline? Is there a new one emerging? I'm almost expecting TAGS to take Jimmy off guard and throw a punch, but something tells me that won't happen. TAGS just isn't that type of guy…but something definitely isn't right here; there wasn't any agreement the fight wasn't happening. Nobody walked into the middle of the ring and declared it void. The dynamic just changed with the arrival of these two idiots – currently pushing a skinhead about and slapping another. What are they thinking? The chubbier one has a really loud voice and sporadically emits drunken burps, before slurping on his beer and excessively wetting the end of his cigarette.

When you watch a horror movie, is it the gory bits that stick in your mind? Or is it the small things: like movements or noises? It's not the fact you know evil is about to jump out; it's the fact you don't know how, or when. And all these little things stick in your mind because they resonate with your own fears.

The strangest thing about events on the field that evening was that they continued to change; they were supposed to be straight forward, but never were. Was Jimmy's fight ever going to materialise, or was it just a precursor for something far worse? Each question only led to another question, because I couldn't comprehend exactly what these two were trying to achieve, and then a repetitive saying kept coming into my head and rolling off my tongue; one that overruled every other. I couldn't help muttering to myself, 'please walk away. Please walk away.'

But they didn't, because why should they? Age was on their side and this was all that mattered. They demanded to know who the ring leader was, so they could dictate what was about to happen next. Having just been told they had interrupted a potentially significant fight because people suspected them to be undercover police, they seemed to think this announcement made them imperious; they were strolling around asking for Jimmy and TAGS as if they were a couple of nobodies, expecting them to get on with it after all, just for their drunken amusement. I'm not exactly sure where this apparent proprietorial state of mind came from, because nobody had actually affirmed it. Maybe it was the alcohol? Maybe it was the uncertainty they so foolishly mistook for respect. Maybe they were so caught up in their moment of attempting to take centre stage they forgot one vital thing: in gangland, you have to earn your place at the top. Age and experience has no bearing on one's quest to take the throne. Word of mouth is what gets you there, and the word of mouth currently moving from person to person is that Darren and Gordon – as they called themselves – were in a huge amount of trouble.

26

The interlopers are weaving in and out the crowd. They can't seem to do so without using physical force; every person greeted with a push or a twist of the ear. Some people give them the time of day, others don't. As I stand watching them push in, speak, then get ignored, I can't help but visualize a small boy lost in a supermarket, searching for his mum; moving through the aisles, shouting out her name, frantically trying to catch the attention of a member of staff, a kind and caring shopper, all the time fighting against the elements, everything around him larger and higher.

I'm not entirely sure what they're asking, and if it's actually anything meaningful or even comprehensible. They're maybe trying to find out the meaning of life. After all, everything we say to a stranger is an attempt to understand the meaning of life. Every time we look in the mirror, every time we open the front door, every time we choose anger over empathy; it's all an attempt to understand the meaning of life.

On occasion they seem to know their place and move on, other times overstaying their welcome and becoming rather unnecessarily aggressive; behaviour apparently depending on how threatened they feel, but with the

Jimmy this, Jimmy that

drink affecting their inhibitions, I wonder how they can actually tell.

Then they try and commandeer the area of grass in-between Jimmy and TAGS, who are amazingly still high in conversation – about something barbaric no doubt – but TAGS effortlessly pushes both of them away, muttering, 'fuck off,' under his breath. The manner in which he avoids confrontation but cements his authority on the situation is impressive. You don't have to fight every battle with a knife. This incongruous, unpredictable relationship forming between Jimmy and TAGS makes me angry at the two uninvited guests, because Jimmy doesn't deserve this amount of respect from someone so highly esteemed. The fact that their arrival has inadvertently gained Jimmy some form of social approval makes me irate and I want to shout out at them and tell them to fuck off also, but how could I possibly do it as elegantly as TAGS?

Then they approach Peebo and his friend, who decide to embrace them with a hug. It's possibly just mockery, but nonetheless, I touch the side of my face, remembering the welcome I got into Peebo's life and wondering if I'm really lower down the social ladder than Darren and Gordon.

I think this is the first time in the evening I've lost sight of Noggin and I start to wonder if he's gone home. As I look around the faces and locate him with some of the other guys from my year, a hand tugs my sleeve. Then the same hand grips my arm. I turn and look at the perpetrator – planning to question his intentions – only to realize it was instinct and he didn't actually want my attention, only my unconditional moral support and understanding. He wanted me to somehow tell him everything was going to be ok.

that

It seems this guy has anticipated the worst and grabbed onto the nearest object available. It's a foreboding grip and I shake him off, looking around me in embarrassment. But then everything goes silent, because there's an almost audible chant coming from the sky, and then it starts to rain.

When you look at the history books and study the great wars – even the less significant ones – there are always statistics about death count, destroyed landmarks, treaties signed by who and what leader, and the post war ramifications on this or that country, but there's never anything about the weather. It never seems to say that a soldier's mobility in the trenches was affected by the rain, or he couldn't tell the difference between the mist and the gas, or the sun in his eyes was his downfall.

The sudden impact of the torrential rain meant everybody looked up to the sky, trying to ascertain why there was a lack of warning from the heavens; everyone except one individual, of course, who took the opportunity to reach into his pocket and extract what looked like a snooker ball in a sock. As the sixty or seventy heads accepted this unrelenting decision from amidst the clouds and brought their eye level back down to horizontal, a great yell sounded through the field.

All of a sudden feet start to move a bit faster and people are trying to work out what's happening, when the other drunkard receives a blow on the back of the head and stumbles, trying to mumble something in his defence but only receiving another punch to the side of the face. Suddenly I have the image of greyhounds at a racecourse and how well behaved they are whilst walking to their traps. This is because they're still on their leash and the rabbit isn't anywhere in sight. The moment the rabbit flies round the corner they're liberated and given permission to demolish this animal.

So whilst these two idiots are trying to get to their feet and look for a means of escape, they forget to take into account that this crowd of young people are just like greyhounds waiting for the rabbit. Just like the dogs – who are used for the purpose of betting and starved so they're thin enough to fly round the track – most of the people in proximity to these two guys aren't exactly content with their desolate lifestyles and lack of opportunity, so having just been given permission to attack aren't likely to decline.

Almost in sync, we charge, trapdoors open, bate at the ready, a whole plethora of weapons suddenly materialising out of nowhere. There's shouting, swearing, kicking, punching, adrenaline rushing madness; everyone is trying to get in on this historic moment, when these two silly bastards imagined they could mess with the youth. They thought they could challenge the systematic organisation of fighting amongst Edinburgh's most feared gang members. Even the weakest among us wants to play a part; wants to get involved, because how can seventy people realistically be blamed for the murder of two individuals?

The barbaric incident only lasted about a minute, but time has no relevance on overall effect. Catastrophes never usually take longer than a few seconds and how long would it realistically take to inflict eternal damage on a couple of lowlifes anyway?

And then the rain stops, and another noise suddenly emerges: the all too familiar noise of a police siren, and that's when we scatter. That's when we come back down to earth and realise what we've been involved in, sprinting in all four directions and running for our lives. Every step we take thinking about our involvement and whether we could be the predominant reason for the imminent arrival of an ambulance.

And then I notice Noggin in front of me and he's stopped at a street corner to take a breath, frantically looking over his shoulder and all around him. I slow down to a jog and stop beside him. He looks into my eyes and I look into his. There's no exchange of words because what can we say? And then Noggin glances down at my hand and his eyes widen. He looks at me as I throw something into the nearest garden, and then looks away. He leans against a fence and looks at me again. He's attempting to ask me something with his eyes, but chooses to go no further with his investigation. He decides against exploring those thoughts racing through his head, because maybe it was right.

Maybe it was how it was supposed to happen.